Guardian's Wrath

Anna Gabriel Book 2

Georgia Wagner

Text Copyright © 2024 Georgia Wagner

Publisher: Greenfield Press Ltd

The right of Georgia Wagner to be identified as author of the Work has been asserted in accordance with the Copyright, Designs and Patents Act 1988

All rights reserved.

The book is copyright material and must not be copied, reproduced, transferred, distributed, leased, licensed or publicly performed or used in any way except as specifically permitted in writing by the publishers, as allowed under the terms and conditions under which it was purchased or as strictly permitted by applicable copyright law. Any unauthorised distribution or use of this text may be a direct infringement of the author's and publisher's rights and those responsible may be liable in law accordingly.

'Guardian's Wrath' is a work of fiction. Names, characters, businesses, organisations, places, events, and incidents either are the product of the author's imagination or are used fictitiously. Any resemblance to actual persons, living or dead, and events or locations is entirely coincidental.

Contents

1. Prologue — 1
2. Chapter 1 — 12
3. Chapter 2 — 26
4. Chapter 3 — 37
5. Chapter 4 — 44
6. Chapter 5 — 55
7. Chapter 6 — 65
8. Chapter 7 — 83
9. Chapter 8 — 95
10. Chapter 9 — 103
11. Chapter 10 — 114
12. Chapter 11 — 125
13. Chapter 12 — 136

14.	Chapter 13	144
15.	Chapter 14	159
16.	Chapter 15	168
17.	Chapter 16	172
18.	Chapter 17	183
19.	Chapter 18	190
20.	Chapter 19	198
21.	Chapter 20	209
22.	Chapter 21	216
23.	Chapter 22	221
24.	What's Next for Anna Gabriel?	228
25.	Also by Georgia Wagner	230
26.	Also by Georgia Wagner	232
27.	Also by Georgia Wagner	234
28.	Want to know more?	236
29.	About the Author	238

Prologue

Jacinth's mind clawed its way back to consciousness, her eyelids fluttering open with effort. A deep throb pulsed through her skull. She tried to lift her hand to the epicenter of pain, only to hear the clink of metal against stone. Her wrist was tethered by a looping chain.

The darkness enveloped her but as the seconds ticked by, faint slivers of light began to carve out the grim details of her prison. She was in a basement, the air musty and stagnant, the walls weeping moisture that gave the shadows an oily sheen. Jacinth's breaths came in shallow gasps as panic pricked at her skin, each inhalation laced with dust from the basement.

Where the hell was she?

Why couldn't she remember... She blinked, trying to manage the darkness.

Her eyes, now adjusting to the scarce light, found purchase on two silhouettes shackled across from her. The first woman sat with her head bowed, resignation etched into the slump of her shoulders. But it was the second figure that drew Jacinth's attention—the source of heart-wrenching sobs that cut through the oppressive silence.

Tears streamed down the second woman's face, glinting in the dimness as she pulled futilely at the chains that bound her to the damp wall. Her cries echoed off the stone and back into Jacinth's already frayed senses.

The realization that she was not alone in this nightmare brought a bitter comfort to Jacinth, yet the sight of the sobbing woman's despair only chilled her.

Where was she? How had she ended up here?

Jacinth shifted against the cold, unyielding floor, her chains clinking softly in the quiet room. Trying to steady her breathing, she closed her eyes, and like a projector flickering to life, images of her family home in Washington State danced behind her eyelids. The towering pines that whispered on the wind, the sprawling fields of lavender that waved under the Pacific Northwest sun, the laughter of her younger siblings as they chased each other around the farmhouse—all of it crashed over her with an ache so profound, it was as if her heart were trying to claw its way back to those simpler times.

The vibrant campus life at her university materialized in her mind next; the thrill of intellectual debates, the pride of aced exams, the camaraderie of late-night study sessions. Jacinth had thrived there, her passion for forensic psychology becoming a north star that guided her every choice.

As the thoughts swirled, a darker memory surfaced, tainting the nostalgia—a memory of just hours before. The date. A charming smile across the table, engaging conversation that made her laugh genuinely, a connection that sparked interest. And then, the drink.

His insistence she try his favorite cocktail, the strange aftertaste that had made her tongue tingle unnervingly. The room spinning, her body growing heavy, the world tilting on its axis until darkness claimed her.

Horror seeped into her bones as the realization fully took hold. Drugged. She'd been drugged.

Jacinth's breath hitched, the cold air of the basement biting at her lungs. Then, another memory. The woman—the calm one. Her name was... Maddie? No... Melody. She'd introduced herself earlier... No. No, Jacinth had heard the name as she'd drifted in and out of consciousness. Melody. The woman's name was Melody.

And even now, Melody remained calm, chained to the wall, but watching the stairs attentively.

Suddenly, voices echoed from above.

She went still, arms shifting, the cold metal of the bindings biting into her wrists.

Suddenly, the unmistakable sound of boots on wooden stairs. Heavy, deliberate, each step a drumbeat heralding a threat drawing ever closer. Jacinth's eyes darted to the staircase, where slivers of light teased the edges of each descending boot, casting long shadows that seemed to reach out towards them like fingers.

One of the other chained women stifled a sob, shrinking back against the wall as if trying to melt into the stone itself. Jacinth's heart raced, pounding a frenetic tempo against her ribs. She had faced fear before—late-night study sessions, walking alone on campus—but nothing like this. This was not the anxiety of deadlines or the wariness of shadows; this was primal, visceral terror.

Amidst the rising tide of fear, a voice cut through the gloom—a whisper tempered with authority.

"Listen to me," the woman spoke, her tone low and steady in the dark. Melody, the third captive whose presence had been a silent shadow until now, shifted within the sliver of light leaking from above.

The sobbing woman didn't quiet. Jacinth stared. This woman was a couple years older, with severe, stern features.

"I said listen," Melody repeated.

"What's the point?" moaned the third captive. Jacinth couldn't remember the weeping woman's name. "They're going to... to kill us."

"No, shh, shh... quiet, please," said Melody.

Jacinth stared at her. She seemed so calm, so in control.

Melody hesitated, biting her lip, and then, suddenly, she spoke quickly, as if deciding it was her only option. "I'm with the FBI. I'm undercover. We're going to get out, but you have to do exactly as I say."

The words seemed surreal, a lifeline thrown in a sea of darkness. Melody's eyes, two points of determination, met Jacinth's.

Beside them, the sobbing woman whimpered, her despair a sharp contrast to Melody's composure. "We can't... they'll hear us," she gasped between sobs, her voice ragged with terror.

"Shh," Melody soothed, her gaze never wavering from Jacinth's. "Trust me. Panic will only make things worse. Stay quiet, stay alert. Do exactly as I say. Can you do that?"

Jacinth nodded, the pain in her head pulsing with each beat of her heart. She focused on Melody's instructions, feeling the ember of her own resolve flare just a bit brighter. In Melody's measured confidence, there was something infectious, a calm that beckoned Jacinth to rise above the panic that clawed at her insides.

"Good," Melody continued, her eyes scanning their surroundings, assessing. "When the time comes, we move quickly. No hesitation."

"Okay," Jacinth whispered back, the word a shard of glass in her dry throat.

Melody gave a curt nod, acknowledging Jacinth's silent commitment. The third, crying woman's sobs had softened into quiet hiccups, the sound almost lost beneath the echo of those relentless footsteps above.

The sudden clamor of the door slamming against the wall shattered the silence, sending a shiver down Jacinth's spine. A shaft of harsh light spilled into the basement, casting long, sinister shadows that clawed their way towards the huddled captives. Figures loomed in the doorway at the top of the stairs, their silhouettes monstrous against the backlight, before they began their descent. The wooden steps groaned under the weight of the men, each thud a drumbeat to impending doom.

Jacinth's heart hammered in her chest as she watched the men approach, with Melody's earlier words echoing in her mind like a mantra: stay alert, no hesitation. But nothing could have prepared her for the sight—or stench—of the figure who detached himself from the group and stalked towards them.

He was scruffy and wild-looking, his greasy hair hanging in matted clumps around a face twisted with rage. The odor that emanated from him was a pungent mix of sweat and something far more foul, an assault on the senses that made Jacinth's stomach churn. The man paced back and forth like a caged animal, his voice rising to a fever pitch as he spat accusations at them.

"Secrets, all of you! Whispering, plotting behind my back!" His eyes were bloodshot, wide with paranoia as they darted between the women. When his gaze landed on Melody, it lingered with a particular venom. "Especially you, FBI," he sneered, his lip curling in disgust. "Thought you could fool us?"

Jacinth's breath caught in her throat as she witnessed the fury directed at Melody, who remained statuesque, her expression betraying none of the fear that must have been roiling within her. The man's pacing grew more frenetic, his tirade punctuated by violent gestures that made the chains clank ominously against the stone walls.

"Promises made, promises broken," he continued, his voice a corrosive hiss that seemed to fill every corner of the basement. "Did you really think we wouldn't find out? Did you think we're that stupid?"

The other women recoiled, but Melody held his gaze unflinchingly, her jaw set in a line of defiance that seemed to infuriate the man even further. He leaned in close to her, his breath a hot gust of malice.

Melody's muscles coiled, a spring wound tight with pent-up energy. Her eyes, hard as flint, tracked the man pacing before them. The rancid air in the basement quivered with tension, every breath a prelude to chaos. Jacinth's pulse hammered in her ears, a drumbeat of impending action.

In a blur of motion, Melody twisted her wrists, the faintest glimmer of metal reflecting in the dim light revealing a concealed metal wire. With a practiced flick, her chains fell away, clattering against the cold concrete floor. Before the echo of rattling metal could die down, she was on her feet and lunging toward the nearest captor.

The man, caught off-guard by the sudden assault, stumbled backward, his hands instinctively reaching for the weapon holstered at his side. But Melody was faster. Her hand shot out, fingers wrapping around his wrist with vice-like precision, wrenching his arm upwards. His grunt of surprise was cut short as Melody's elbow slammed into his face, a crunch of cartilage breaking the heavy silence.

Jacinth watched, wide-eyed and frozen, as Melody wrested the gun from the man's limp grip. A desperate scuffle broke out, a tangled dance of limbs and survival instinct. Melody maneuvered with a fluidity that betrayed her training, her movements sharp and decisive. The other captors hesitated, their shouts turning to confusion as they scrambled to react to the whirlwind that had been unleashed upon them.

The basement erupted into pandemonium, but at its eye stood Melody, now armed and exuding a dangerous calm. She pivoted, the gun steady in her grasp, as she assessed the situation, ready to turn the tide of their grim captivity. For a moment, the balance of power teetered, precariously tilting in favor of the women whose fates had been so uncertain mere seconds before.

Jacinth's heart soared.

The scruffy man's eyes never wavered, his gaze locked on Melody with a cold, calculating stare that belied the chaos around him. His nose bleeding, he didn't seem to even notice. As if on cue, his hand delved into the pocket of his stained jeans, fishing out a battered cell phone. He flipped it open with a practiced motion, thumbing the keypad with an eerie calmness.

"Armin," he barked into the receiver, his voice void of emotion. "Tell me," the scruffy man said, his tone dangerously low, "how much do you think your partner's life is worth, Agent?"

Melody's posture faltered for a split second, the gun lowering just a fraction as her face contorted with horror. It was a moment's hesitation, but it spoke volumes.

"Talk to him," the scruffy man demanded, extending the phone towards Melody, a cruel smirk tugging at the corners of his lips. "He doesn't sound too comfortable."

With a trembling hand, Melody reached for the phone, her fingers brushing against the cold plastic. The gun dipped further.

"Armin?" Melody's voice cracked as she pressed the phone to her ear, the name barely a whisper but charged with a raw desperation that resonated in the tight space.

"Enough," the scruffy man snapped, snatching back the phone and cutting off the connection. "You know what you need to do."

Jacinth watched as Melody's resolve crumbled, the gun finally dropping to her side in a gesture of defeat.

Jacinth's heart pounded as the men seized Melody by the arms. The basement air, already thick with despair, seemed to constrict further, squeezing the hope from Jacinth's lungs with each labored breath.

"Let me go!" Melody's voice was a strangled mix of outrage and resignation, her body thrashing against the men's unyielding hold. But her strength, so palpable moments before, was no match for their brutish force.

The sobbing woman across from Jacinth let out a choked whimper, her eyes wide and shimmering with tears that reflected the scant light trickling down from the stairwell. She tugged futilely at her chains, the metal clinking.

Jacinth tried to speak, to shout encouragement or some semblance of a plan, but her throat was tight, the words trapped.

The group retreated up the wooden stairs as Jacinth watched in horror. The sound of her scuffling and the men's gruff commands faded, leaving behind a hollow echo.

Silence crashed down upon the basement like a verdict, punctuated only by the other woman's quiet sobs and the distant thud of a door slamming shut.

Chapter 1

"Again," Anna snapped.

She watched as her younger sister flung a combination of punches at the man in the ring. He blocked most of them, absorbed one on his chin and retaliated with an uppercut of his own.

Beth's head snapped back, her blonde hair whipping across her pale features. She stumbled, gasped, and tried to block in anticipation of a return punch.

Beth's opponent hesitated, shooting Anna a quick glance. His head was shaved and he now boasted a thick beard, giving him the look of a bouncer at a night-club. The tattoos up and down his muscular arms only further added to the intimidating effect. But he had kind eyes, and his posture was one of reluctance.

Casper, her old SEAL buddy, wore thick, twelve ounce gloves. He was also pulling his punches—he didn't want to hurt Beth. But this misplaced compassion was costing Anna's sister in the long run.

Anna hadn't wanted to train her baby sister. For two months, she'd flat-out refused. But Beth had been persuasive, and Anna had given her word.

"Dammit!" Anna shouted. "Again!"

Casper sighed, shifting in the ring. These constant training sessions had helped the ex-SEAL shed some of the puppy weight he'd taken on after his retirement. Three months ago, he'd been round of belly and ruddy of cheek. Now, he looked lean again, and the work with free weights was evident in his physique.

Anna brushed the single shock of white hair behind her ear, one scarred hand tensed at her side. She stood just outside the makeshift boxing ring in the abandoned industrial complex where they'd set up shop. Anna's green eyes surveyed the scene, her expression impassive, as she often kept her emotions like cards close to the chest. If not for the tattoo on her forearm, some might have mistaken her for a good church girl; minimal makeup, a simple pony-tail, pleasant features.

But three tours on two continents working as a government assassin undermined the apparent image. Plus, she was now instructing her old friend to beat up her baby sister.

This last part troubled Anna most of all, but as the old saying went: no pain, no gain.

Beth was bleeding from her nose, her lip. She trembled, shaking her head, staring at the ground, her hands at her side.

"Beth, again!" Anna said. "It's not done."

Beth just stood there, shaking and staring at the ground.

"Beth!"

Casper glanced at her, fist cocked. Anna nodded once, but Casper shook his head. Anna scowled. "Do it—round's not over."

But Casper stepped back, crossing his arms and glaring at her. "This is bullshit, Anna."

Beth looked up now, her face tense, her voice shaking. "I didn't pay you to stop!" The stay-at-home mother of two had a fierce look in her eyes. She glared from Casper to Anna and back again. "I can take it. I can!"

"There's a difference between training and punishing yourself," Casper muttered.

Beth looked at him, tense. Her features were like those of a cheerleader, and Anna had often felt her sister was the prettier of the two. Anna's own features were passably attractive with sea green eyes, an upturned nose, sharp cheekbones and a shock of white through raven-black hair.

But the tattoos of the bone-frog carrying the trident on her forearm placed her firmly outside the vector of "good girls" world round.

Beth, on the other hand, had been the prototypical good girl. She'd graduated Summa Cum Laude from university, had married young, often volunteered at church groups and raised her kids with a loving husband.

But all of that had been stripped away.

Anna pictured the flash of orange, the explosion of the helicopter.

All three of Beth's family members had been purported to be on that helicopter. But Beth held out hope that they were still alive.

Anna wasn't so sure. She'd played through that fateful night again and again in her mind, and each time she reached the same conclusion: Beth's family, as tragic as it was, had died. But she didn't have the heart to rip away this small, sliver of hope. And so when Beth had insisted Anna train her, teach her... Anna hadn't been able to refuse.

In Beth's mind, if she could learn the same skills Anna had, then she could help find and rescue her family. Anna and Casper had already been scouring their network of sources. No one had spotted the albino—the man who'd kidnapped Beth. No one had heard of Tom, Sarah or Tony being alive anywhere.

Anna let out a faint sigh, shaking her head again. "That's enough for today," she said wearily, rubbing a hand across her brow.

Casper was still standing in the ring, arms crossed.

"No," Beth insisted. She pointed at Casper. "I paid you the insurance money from our home. You can't stop. Not now. A deal is a deal."

Casper winced, his kind eyes bunching up. Normally, the ex-SEAL had an aloof quality to his posture and words, as if he couldn't quite be bothered to care about much of anything... ever. Except for his car—Casper cared a helluva lot about his car. Anna still didn't know what make and model it was. A hail cat? Hellcat? No... wait, a Dodge something? She couldn't be bothered to remember.

The look in Casper's eyes currently directed at Beth was a look he normally reserved for the engine block of his vehicle; he studied Beth with a mix of pity and empathy. Anna watched as Casper's resolve crumbled, his broad shoulders falling in defeat.

With a heavy sigh, Casper nodded and stepped back into position, his gloves raised.

"Alright," Casper said, his voice gruff. "One more round."

Beth's eyes lit up with determination as she squared her shoulders, wiping the blood from her face with the back of her glove. She took a deep breath and raised her fists, ready to continue the relentless training session.

As the training resumed, Anna couldn't help but feel a sense of dread creeping over her. She knew that delving deeper into the dangerous world they were stepping into would only lead to more heartache and turmoil.

For nearly four weeks now, they'd trained. Twice a day. Anna hadn't accepted a single penny of Beth's insurance money, preferring to sleep in her RV behind the gym rather than bleed any of Beth's funds, but she'd also been the one to convince Beth that if her sister was serious about learning the tools of the trade, then Casper was the best of the best. Hiring him was an investment.

Beth hadn't taken much convincing, and neither had Casper. Two ex-wives had taken their toll on his bank account.

As the final round continued, Anna called out. "Be right back. Gonna grab a bite!"

She didn't wait to see if either of them had heard. She sauntered away from the ring, her eyes scanning the old, abandoned structure. Meticulously documenting the cameras she'd placed throughout the ceiling joists, the small alarm box Casper had installed by the garage door, and the two stashes of weapons hidden in alcoves near old support beams.

All of this—double and triple-checking—was second nature to her.

The faint chill down her spine, as if someone was always watching, also came with the territory. She was used to it.

She stepped out of the old building, and into the fresh, afternoon air. The wind swelled through the trees surrounding the picturesque Mammoth Lake, gently rustling the leaves and carrying the soft scent of pine. Anna took in a deep breath, letting the crisp air fill her lungs as she strolled along the lake's edge. The sky above was a brilliant canvas of blue, dotted with fluffy white clouds that drifted lazily in the breeze.

As she walked, her mind drifted back to Beth and Casper in the training ring. She couldn't shake off the feeling of unease that had settled in her chest. Beth's determination was admirable, but Anna feared that her sister was diving headfirst into a world she knew nothing about.

Suddenly, a twig snapped behind her, jolting Anna out of her thoughts. She spun around, her hand instinctively reaching for the concealed knife strapped to her thigh.

Another crack. A branch?

She frowned, frozen, motionless. Anna didn't twitch. As a sniper, she'd learned the skill of staying very, very still. In this age of thirty-second videos and instant gratification, the art of remaining motionless, without entertainment, for hours, sometimes days, was a rarity. Sometimes, the twitch of a hand or the shift of a foot was the difference between life and death.

And so she remained poised, motionless, watching, scanning, searching.

And then more sounds. Whoever it was didn't care if they were heard.

A second later, a figure stumbled out from the treeline, gasping and moaning.

Standing a few paces away was a man she didn't recognize. The man stumbled towards her, mouth opening and closing like a fish. He gasped in her direction and let out a faint mewl of pain as he hit his knees.

"H-help," he stammered. And then he keeled over, clutching at his stomach.

It was only then she spotted the knife.

Anna rushed forward to the fallen man, her heart pounding in her chest. She knelt beside him, quickly assessing his condition. Blood seeped through his shirt where the knife had found its mark, and Anna knew she had to act fast. With practiced hands, she tore a strip of cloth from her own shirt and applied pressure to the wound, trying to stem the bleeding.

"What happened?" Anna asked urgently, scanning their surroundings for any potential threats. The man groaned in response, his eyes squeezing shut in pain.

He tried to speak, but his voice faltered.

"Hey, hey!" she yelled. "Stay with me. Stay with..." But she trailed off. Too late. Clearly too late. He'd lost too much blood.

She stared at the man's face.

His eyes fluttered open, and for a moment, they locked onto Anna's in a silent plea. Then, with a shuddering breath, his gaze turned distant, unfocused. A flicker of defeat passed through his features before they slackened into stillness. The weight of his final exhale hung heavy in the air, mingling with the scent of pine and earth.

"Shit," she whispered. She stared down at the man, stunned.

It all happened so fast. But that was the real world. Fast. Unpredictable. She moved just as quickly into assessing phase.

Assess the threat. Neutralize the enemy.

Glancing around warily once more, Anna's instincts hummed with caution. She hoisted herself to her feet, but instead of turning back to the gym, she moved in the direction the man had come from.

He'd been stabbed. Were his killers nearby? She had to localize the threat, first.

And involving Beth?

No. Not at this stage. Hopefully never.

Even as she moved through the woods, over the carpet of detritus and pine needles, her hand strayed for her phone. She noticed blood staining her fingers, and she wiped them against a moss covered log. As she pulled her phone with her preferred left hand, she frowned. Still no notifications. No warnings that the albino had been spotted. No news of Beth's family.

Was this dead man part of it, somehow?

Her brow furrowed as she moved under the cover of trees, footsteps soft against the padded ground. She spotted motion ahead of her and glanced up. A figure in a gray hood, moving hastily through the trees away from her.

"Hey!" she called out. "Hey, stop!"

But the figure didn't look back.

Anna frowned, beginning to jog, but then she stumbled, and turned sharply to stare at the forested floor.

And that's when she found the second body.

She blinked, staring.

A woman this time. Laying on the mossy earth, wearing a dark suit. A knife buried in her throat. Her eyes stared up at the clouds, glassy.

"What the hell?" Anna murmured under her breath.

She dropped to a knee, reaching out and touching the woman's skin. Cold. She rifled through this woman's pockets and found a billfold. Inside, she found something that made her curse.

An FBI badge.

"Shit," she whispered, dropping the item and stumbling back. She shot a look over her shoulder, rapidly trying to make sense of the situation.

Was the man the one who'd killed the woman? Had she fought back?

No... no, that didn't make sense. The man's stab wound was from a left-handed person. This woman was clearly right-handed, judging by the callouses on her fingers and the hand she'd gripped at the knife in her throat with.

All of this information flooded her brain on instinct and training alone. A left-handed killer... Shit. Double shit. She glanced at her own hand, and suddenly realized she needed to leave now. She cursed, turning on her heel, but before she could move, a voice called out.

"Hands up! Get your goddamn hands up!"

She froze in place, glancing back. A man was emerging from the treeline, gun in hand, pointing at her head.

Two more men flanked him.

All of them wore black suits. All of them carried dark scowls. "Get on the ground!" one of them shouted.

She tensed, assessing the situation. They were drawing close. The trees could provide cover if she decided to make a move. She didn't speak yet.

Were these the killers?

But before this thought had even completed its circuit through her synapses, one of the other figures let out a howl—not a man after all. The shaved head had thrown her for a loop, but the figure was distinctly feminine. This woman surged towards the fallen form on the ground. "Melody!" she yelled, her voice full of pain. "You killed Melody!"

The man holding the gun on her scowled. The safety clicked off. "Where's Armin?" he demanded. "Where is he! Tell us now. Did you kill him too?"

Anna blinked, swallowed faintly, and glanced over her shoulder. The trail of blood would be easy enough to follow. At least she now had the names of the two murder victims.

But by the looks of things, these three suited folk were FBI.

And by the sound of things, they had their primary suspect in the murders.

"On the ground! I said get on the ground, dammit!"

Reluctantly, she lowered slowly. "I didn't do this."

"Shut up! Get down!"

She let out a faint, frustrated sigh, lowering herself to the ground, her face pressed against pine needles, inhaling the scent of earth. A shout from behind her indicated the second body had been found.

And though she lay on moss and leaves, she felt as if she'd just gotten herself into a giant pile of crap.

Chapter 2

"I didn't kill them," Anna said, her voice cold as her eyes darted around the dark van.

Her hands were cuffed behind her back as she calmly surveyed the FBI agents across from her. The man who'd pulled the gun was there, along with the bald woman.

Both of them stared back at her, sitting in plastic chairs across from the picnic table between them in this mobile interrogation unit. A Sprinter van, judging by the wheel wells—not wide enough to be a Promaster. Anna catalogued this information—it wasn't a conscious effort, but rather the result of her subconscious processing any small piece of information that might give her an advantage. Her wrists chaffed against the cuffs, and her eyes flicked between her two captors.

How many times had she been on the other side of the table? How many times had she been involved during CIA's advanced interrogation techniques?

She'd been hunting bad guys. That's how she'd always seen it.

Anna didn't believe in living under the shadow of regret. The past haunted only those who willingly exhumed the bones of bad decisions but her mind flitted to Yemen. She pictured a Middle Eastern man with a thick, brown beard. He'd stared at her with the same intensity as the FBI agents. He'd cursed at her in Arabic. At first, she'd thought he was innocent, but then she'd spotted the scar. The same scar as the bomber in the bazaar. The same scar as the gunman who'd opened fire on her teammates.

She shivered, closing her eyes, weathering the storm of the unbidden memory. PTSD, some called it. She could hear the echo of gunshots, the loud blast. The screaming women. The crying children. The shouting men.

Hellfire had rained down on that bazaar, and the hunt for the perpetrators had eventually led her being dishonorably discharged.

It's never a good sign when the government tells a would-be assassin to pack their bags, but the CO she'd punched had leverage, and she'd been shown the door.

And now here she sat, facing two suits wearing similar expressions of cold anger. Clearly, they knew the victims.

"I didn't kill them," she repeated. "I just found them."

"Right," said the man with the handlebar moustache. "Because you were boxing in that old building? Hmm?"

"Like I told you."

"You said two others would be there. They're not."

Anna nodded, mildly impressed. Casper was good. He'd likely seen the suits on the security cameras and snuck out the back with Beth. She felt a flicker of relief knowing Casper was with her little sister. There were few people she'd trust with Beth's life. In fact, only one other. And that person was currently cuffed in the back of a moving van.

She surveyed the two FBI agents. The man with the handlebar moustache looked to be middle-aged with salt-and-pepper hair along with a no-nonsense attitude. He reminded her of a stern substitute teacher. His suit looked more like a uniform, and his posture suggested a military background. Army. Definitely not Navy. She knew her own kind, and this one wasn't it.

The female partner was frowning at Anna, and there was something far more personal in her glare, as if she wanted to lunge across the table and rip Anna to pieces. This woman would have been beautiful if she'd spent ten seconds tending to her appearance, but clearly she had different priorities. No makeup. Lumpy ear on the left side, suggesting she had a combat sport background. Head shaved completely. Suit unbuttoned at the top, but no jewelry. Her dark skin was flawless—no tattoos, no markings, no scars of any kind. Save the knuckles.

Definitely a combat sport background.

Agent Greeves and Agent Jefferson.

She glanced at Greeves, Mr. Handlebar, and said in that usual, laconic way of hers, "I found them like that."

"We found you handling their bodies," said Greeves slowly. "We found this on your person." He reached behind the table and withdrew her thigh-strap knife, placing it on the surface between them.

His eyebrows inched up as if he were projecting the thought Aha!

She shrugged. "My knife is clean. Should show I didn't stab 'em."

"You're left-handed," said Greeves.

"Mhmm."

"You killed them, bitch!" snapped Jefferson. The woman lunged across the table, grabbing a handful of Anna's collar, gripping tight. "I'll make sure you fry for this. Hear me?"

Anna didn't react to the manhandling. She waited patiently until Greeves pried his partner's hand free from Anna's collar. Jefferson stood to her feet, pacing back and forth now. She was nearly six feet in height, and she moved like a caged bull waiting to be let loose.

"Fiancé?" said Anna quietly.

Jefferson turned to her, rage in her eyes.

"Which one?" Anna asked. "Him? He asked me for help. I was trying to find who did this. That's all."

Jefferson continued to pace. Anna supposed she'd guessed correctly, judging by the murderous glare in the FBI agent's expression. Greeves looked frustrated by the situation, and she wondered why he was allowing his partner to remain in the interrogation. She was clearly emotionally distraught.

"Tell us what you know about the case our colleagues were working," Greeves said simply, folding his hands.

"Nothing. Like I said, I didn't hurt them."

"They just stumbled into a left-handed knife user in the woods. Is that your story?"

"About right," Anna said simply. She glanced around the van. They were motionless on the side of the road. Two more agents were up front, waiting for orders. Four to one—not great odds.

Especially with her hands cuffed. But she waited, watched, gathering intel before executing.

Beth was safe. Priority one accomplished.

But now... now the feds seemed to think she had killed their agents. Not good. She hesitated, picturing the fleeing, grey-hooded figure she'd spotted back in the forest.

"I saw someone," she said simply.

"Oh? Convenient!" Jefferson snapped.

"Who?" asked Greeves. "Didn't see their face."

"Can you describe them?"

"Not really. Hooded. Running away from the crime scene."

Greeves and Jefferson exchanged glances, skepticism etched on their faces. Greeves leaned back in his chair, looking at Anna with a mixture of disbelief and suspicion.

"You saw someone running away from the crime scene, but you don't know their face or anything about them? That seems... highly unlikely," he said.

Anna's eyes narrowed. She knew exactly what he was doing. He was trying to make her feel small, to break her down. But she wasn't about to let that happen.

"Is that all you're going to say?" cut in Jefferson, her voice thick with anger. "She's got nothing but lies."

Anna could see the tension in their faces, the desperation in their eyes. She'd seen that look before, back when she was in the field, when they were hunting the same monsters she was.

"Look," she said, her voice soft but firm. "I'm not lying. I found those agents. I didn't kill them."

Greeves sighed, rubbing a hand over his face. "So who the hell are you, then? Hmm? No prints. No social security number. No driver's license." He looked at her.

She sighed, glancing at the table before looking up again. "I don't believe in voluntarily registering into some system. I know how easy it is to get lose in the numbers."

"No credit cards?"

"I don't believe in plastic." Or money, she thought to herself. She had never much seen the use in money. She didn't trust it, and often gave it away as quickly as she got it. Gold? Gold she could touch. Could feel. She had gold hidden in the walls of her C-class RV.

"I need to go," she said simply. "I've sat here, tried to help. But you're clearly not in a reasoning mood." Her eyes shifted to Jefferson. "I'm sorry about what happened to your fiancé. Your colleague. But I'm done."

"Done?" snapped Jefferson. "Is that how you think this works? What sort of asshole are you?"

Greeves leaned forward now. "Do you work for Abdo Sahid? Is he the one who sent you?"

She stared at Greeves now.

"Bingo," Jefferson said. "We know about your boss, bitch. We know who hired you."

"Hang on... Sahid is involved in this?" Anna asked, leaning forward now. She'd been tensed, prepared to make her move. She'd nearly slipped her thumb free from the cuffs. She'd been preparing to sweep Greeves' chair leg then lunge at Jefferson before she had time to react.

But now, Anna tensed, hesitant.

"You work for him?" Greeves pressed.

"No." But I tried to kill his nephew once, Anna thought to herself. She frowned. One of her first missions for the black ops team. A target on a human-trafficker. One of the most prolific traffickers with operations in Southern Africa and the Middle East. Everyone on her squad had known the name Abdo Sahid.

She knew many names—all of them belonging to nasty people. But Abdo Sahid was a particularly repugnant specimen: a sadist, a psychopath, a man who had managed to build one of the largest human trafficking empires in the world. But Anna had never actually met him, never seen his face in person. The'd been in the business of eliminating men like Sahid, not making deals with the devil. Still, the mention of Sahid's name sent a shiver down her spine.

She'd missed that first shot at his nephew. But his car had veered off and he'd died in the hospital six months later. A half success. The bosses had been fine with it, and Anna had been moved on to other targets. Especially those involved in disruption and terrorism. It was the same quandry the US had faced when pulling out of Afghanistan. The Afghani officials in the secularized government were known for taking on Tea-boys. Adolescents they severely abused. The marines on the ground were required, in some instances, to look the other way. On one hand, the threat of a dangerous regime, on the other, moral depravity.

Geo politics had never been Anna's strong suit, but it had often bothered her: going after the political sorts, and leaving the scum of the earth to ply their trades in the secret corners.

She bit on her lower lip. "I don't work for anyone. Not anymore. And I didn't kill your agents."

"Enough," Jefferson spat. "This is bullshit. Complete bullshit. She's not—"

"Boss!" a voice suddenly crackled over the speakers in the back.

Anna glanced up at the device set in the ceiling.

"Yeah?" Greeves replied.

"Found something on the drone," the voice said. "Man fleeing on foot. Gray hoodie. Just like she said."

Greeves shot her a look. Jefferson went quiet.

"How far?" Greeves called out.

"Two miles."

"Can we intercept?"

"Yeah. Hold on to something."

Anna tensed as the van's engine suddenly grumbled to life. The vehicle began to move, carrying her even further away from her sister. Her stomach tightened as they picked up speed.

Chapter 3

The world outside the tinted windows of the FBI van blurred into a spinning kaleidoscope of greens and grays as the vehicle careened off the pavement, its tires screeching a violent protest. Anna's stomach lurched with the momentum. Within the confined space, every rattle and jolt was magnified, resonating through the metal bench that served as her temporary seat.

The van skidded to a gritty halt, dust from the roadside uprising in a cloud around them.

"Stay put," Agent Greeves barked, his hand instinctively reaching for the sidearm holstered at his hip. The command was unnecessary; they both knew Anna wasn't going anywhere—yet. He threw a glance at Jefferson, a silent exchange passing between them before he wrenched the back door open. Daylight flooded in, momentarily blinding, and Greeves wasted no time in springing out into the fray.

Anna listened to the gravel crunch under his boots as he took off in the hunt for the man in the gray hoodie.

Jefferson moved to follow her partner, but paused, shooting a glare back at Anna. She reached towards her belt.

The metallic clink of the handcuffs echoed in the tight space as Jefferson, her bald head glistening under the van's dull interior light, loomed over Anna. Without a word, she yanked Anna's ankles together, the cuffs snapping shut.

Anna met Jefferson's eyes, noting the hard set of her jaw and the slight flare of her nostrils — silent tells of disdain. Despite the animosity emanating from the agent, Anna remained composed. As Jefferson bent to secure the cuffs to the chair's base, Anna, under the guise of shifting uncomfortably, flexed her calves, muscles tautening like coiled springs.

The cuffs strained against her unexpected resistance, the rigid metal grazing along her skin as they slid upwards, inch by imperceptible inch. Anna masked the maneuver with a grimace, feigning discomfort. Jefferson, absorbed in the task, failed to notice.

"Jefferson, I see him!" a voice shouted from further out.

The female agent glanced sharply at the door, exhaling sharply. "Keep still," Jefferson muttered, her attention momentarily diverted by the commotion outside.

With no more than a curt glare toward Anna, Jefferson pivoted on her. The back of the van gaped open like a dark maw as she took off in pursuit of Greeves, her footsteps spraying gravel which *tinged* off the metal of the car.

A distinct set of heavier slams resonated through the vehicle's frame—the front doors. She envisioned the drivers, previously unseen but now an integral part of the chase.

The forest outside erupted into a frenzy of sound, piercing the previously held silence with the intensity of a siren. Shouting voices melded into one another, each cry laced with an urgency. The unmistakable crack of gunshots split the air, quick and sharp, punctuated by the duller thuds of boots pounding against the earth.

With the chaos providing a cover, Anna seized her moment. She exhaled slowly, a deliberate act to calm the adrenaline surging through her veins. Her muscles, tense from anticipation, now relaxed in calculated measure. She shifted subtly, angling her legs downward, feeling the cuffs that had been biting into her skin loosen their grip. The metallic constraints slid along the contour of her calves—down, down, until they encircled her ankles with deceptive ease.

The clink of chain against floorboard was almost lost amidst the external clamor, but to Anna, it was as significant as the final click of a lock disengaging. With this small victory, she found herself unshackled.

Anna's eyes narrowed as she surveyed the interior of the van, each breath a quiet calculation. There was no room for panic. She spied the loose screw beneath the table, its head glinting subtly in the dim light that filtered through the vehicle's barred windows. She stretched her foot, the muscles in her leg coiling and then extending.

With a deft flick of her ankle, she hooked the screw, drawing it closer. The metal was cold against her skin. Working the edge of the screw against the locking mechanism of her handcuffs, she felt the tumblers within begrudgingly give way.

A faint click signaled the release of the handcuffs, and Anna's wrists were free. She allowed herself the ghost of a smile, the gesture fleeting and unseen by anyone but the shadows that played hide and seek across the van's interior.

In one fluid motion, she rose from the chair. She approached the back doors with measured strides, her every sense attuned to the world beyond the steel barrier.

Her hand found the door latch, the mechanism yielding without protest. As the doors swung open, a rush of cool air greeted her, carrying with it the earthy scent of pine and soil disturbed by the frenzy of the chase outside. She stepped down onto the uneven ground, her gaze lifting to assess her surroundings.

And then she saw him—a blur of gray against the greenery.

The man in the gray hoodie closed the distance with alarming speed, a glint of steel emerging from the folds of his garment. Likely, he'd spotted the van as a potential getaway vehicle.

Oops. Too bad for him.

Anna's muscles coiled as she registered the threat, her mind already calculating the trajectory of the impending stab.

As he lunged forward, knife aimed for her torso, Anna pivoted to her left with a dancer's grace, the blade slicing only air. She felt the whoosh of its passing, a whisper of danger that failed to find its mark.

With an almost serpentine fluidity, the attacker recovered, thrusting the knife towards her once more, his face hidden beneath the hood but his intentions clear as day. But Anna was ready, her body primed for survival. She caught his wrist with her right hand and anchored herself with her left foot, turning to use his momentum against him.

In one smooth, practiced movement, she twisted beneath his arm, her back pressing against his chest. She used his forward motion to hoist him over her shoulder. The world spun for a fraction of a second - a blend of green and gray - before he crashed to the ground behind her, the knife skittering away into the underbrush.

Breathless but unharmed, Anna stood tall above the prone figure, her stance wide and alert for any further threats.

The assailant lay sprawled on the forest floor, his breath ragged. Anna's gaze flickered to the discarded cuffs, a glint of metal in the dirt. Lunging forward, she snatched them up, her fingers working with practiced efficiency. In one fluid motion, she straddled the man's back, pinning him with her knees. The click of the cuffs closing around his wrists was satisfyingly final.

"Stay down," she murmured.

The sounds of the chase that had unfolded beyond the treeline returned as heavy footsteps signaled an approach. Greeves burst through the underbrush first, gun raised and ready, only to skid to a halt at the sight. Jefferson followed close behind, weapon drawn.

"What the hell?" Greeves managed, his voice a mixture of bewilderment and winded disbelief.

"Secured," Anna said flatly, rising to stand over the subdued attacker, her own breathing measured despite the exertion.

Jefferson lowered her gun, eyes sweeping from Anna to the cuffed man beneath her feet. She let out a long, slow exhale.

"I didn't kill your friends," Anna said, scowling. She nudged the man on the ground with her foot. "But I bet this guy knows who did."

Chapter 4

Now, Anna stood on the same side as the two agents. Jefferson still didn't trust her, evident in her scowl and constant sidelong glances, but for the moment, the two FBI agents had cornered their hooded suspect against the side of their black-paneled van.

She tried to keep her expression passive, but part of her wondered if she simply was *magnetic* to trouble.

She spotted a small droplet of blood on her sleeve which she kept trying to wipe away with a twitching trigger finger. Thankfully, Agent Jefferson hadn't noticed.

Anna stood just to the right of Greeves, watching as the mustachioed fed stepped close to their suspect. The hooded man had wide, froggy eyes set a bit too far apart. His lip was twisted into a perpetual sneer on account of the scar running from his lower lip to his ear. He spat at Greeves, a wild glint in his eyes as he lunged forward.

But Jefferson was faster—her arm shot out like a viper, catching the man's throat in a vice grip. The man struggled, clawing at her with elongated nails that gleamed in the sunlight filtering through the trees.

Anna observed the scene with a detached air, her mind already moving on to what lay beyond this moment.

Jefferson forced the suspect to his knees, his struggles weakening under her unyielding grip. Greeves took a step forward, his gaze flickering between Anna and the man on the ground. The forest seemed to hold its breath, the only sound the rustle of leaves in the gentle breeze.

"Who sent you?" Jefferson's voice was low, a dangerous edge cutting through the stillness of the woods.

The man's eyes darted between the agents and Anna, his chest heaving as he tried to speak through Jefferson's iron hold.

"Talk," Jefferson demanded, tightening her grip even further.

Anna cleared her own throat. "So... can I go now?"

Jefferson shot her an angry look while still wrangling the man. Anna noted he tried to pry at the forearm across his neck with his left hand. She spotted blood speckles on his fingers, and evidence of scratches on his forearm. All of this she catalogued dispassionately, but held her breath, turning to leave.

"Where the hell do you think you're going?" snapped Jefferson.

Greeves shot Anna a look and held up a hand as if to say stay there. She sighed, shaking her head. "Look, I'm ex-military. I'm not one of the bad guys. Got it?"

Greeves paused, turning to look at her. He hesitated briefly. His eyes slipped to the bone frog and trident tattoo on her forearm, then back up to meet her green eyes, the same hue as seas before storm.

"What team?" he said quietly.

She shrugged. "Does it matter?"

"My brother's oldest son is active," Greeves replied.

A strange phrasing; brother's oldest son. Not *nephew*. But she didn't press the point. Anna tensed, glancing from the fed and his large moustache towards the look of suspicion in his narrowed eyes. For a moment, he'd fully turned away from the suspect his partner was wrangling against the side of the van.

Jefferson was busy trying to subdue the wide-eyed man in the gray hoodie while the two other agents were in the front of the van, radioing location and calling for paramedics—the sound of static filled the air along the edge of the empty road framing Mammoth Lakes.

Now, she studied Greeves and said, "I was on special assignment under Corporal Weiso."

"Right... right... based in Senegal?" Greeves asked.

She frowned. "No. Yemen."

He seemed to relax a bit at this, leaning back. He let out a slow exhale. "Shit. You really were Navy?"

"Like I said. Now... can I go?"

He glanced once more towards Jefferson who'd finally managed to subdue their suspect. Then the fed glanced back at her with a sheepish look. "Discharged?"

"Yeah."

"You don't think... you'd wanna stick around a second? See what you get from this guy?" Greeves studied her, grimacing apologetically even as he asked.

She blinked in surprise, hesitated, and then scratched at the side of her face. "This is about Abdo Sahid?"

"Yeah. If you knew him... you know why we need to stop him."

"People have tried for quite some time," she replied.

"Yeah," Greeves said, "But we have reason to believe he's coming here."

"What. To the US?" as she said it, Anna's posture tensed. She felt a flicker of anger flash through her. She remembered all the young women and men who's lives had been ripped apart by Sahid's sex trade. She pictured a scene from memory:

Anna standing in the sand-swept streets of Yemen, the sun beating down mercilessly on her and her team. The mission was clear - infiltrate Sahid's compound and extract the hostages. She could still feel the weight of her gear, the tension in her muscles as they moved as shadows through the night. And then, the chaos - gunfire echoing off the high walls, screams mixing with shouts of command.

Then, first room of the compound, a young girl, barely in her teens, with haunted eyes and bruises marring her skin. An IED strapped to her chest. She'd been used as a human shield.

She hadn't made it out alive.

Anna's teeth pressed together as she snapped back to the present, breathing heavily and glaring at the ground. Finally, she turned away from Greeves and approached the man in the gray hood. She dropped to one knee and reached out, grabbing a fistful of his hair, tilting his head back.

"Hey!" Jefferson snapped. Her hand clapped Anna on the shoulder as if to drag her back.

"It's fine," Greeves said sharply.

Anna ignored the hand on her shoulder. In her experience, only those who didn't actually possess physical skill liked the idea of retaliating against every slight. Thin-skinned folks loved the scene in a movie where the star beat up a few bad guys based on a slight insult. But in Anna's experience, the true killers were the ones who maintained their professionalism and composure.

The hand on her shoulder was just another distraction. Like sand in the surf. Like sunlight on a hot day.

Jefferson and Greeves were now disagreeing behind her, but she ignored them both.

Her eyes were instead fixated on the suspect.

His wide eyes were blinking as he met her gaze. He sat hunched against the hubcap of the van, breathing heavily, his intermittent gasps competing with the static from the radio coming from the front seat.

She didn't speak English. Sahid was Yemeni. And so she spoke to this man in fluent Arabic. "Man 'ant?"

He froze, staring at her. His breath came in slow puffs. She nodded, and continued in Arabic. "You're with Sahid?"

He didn't reply. Didn't react, just maintained his gaze fixated on her.

Anna could see the fear in the man's eyes, but she also recognized the glint of defiance. She didn't have time to waste on mind games. Leaning in closer, she spoke in a low, firm tone in Arabic, "I know who you are and what you do. If you want any chance of survival, start talking now."

The man's eyes darted around, as if contemplating his options. Before he could respond, a crackling voice came through the radio announcing backup units closing in on their location. Anna's sense of urgency heightened.

She tightened her grip on his collar and repeated her question in a steely voice, "Where is Sahid heading? When is he expected to arrive? And what are his plans here?"

The man swallowed hard, beads of sweat forming on his brow. Jefferson was still chirping away, complaining to Greeves. But Anna ignored all of this. She stared at the man in the hood, hesitant. Again, her thoughts drifted back to that scene in Yemen. That young woman, trapped... the beeping sound of the IED...

No... that wasn't memory.

That sound was...

She stared.

Beep. Beep. Beepbeep. It was getting louder.

The man was praying now in Arabic, muttering rapidly under his breath. Anna's eyes widened. "Get back!" she yelled. She shoved Greeves and Jefferson. There was no visible external sign of an explosive on the murder suspect. Which meant... it was internal.

Shit.

She flung herself back, tackling Greeves. Out of the van—the two of them hit the dust, behind the silver bumper. The beeping grew even louder. "Alahu Ackbar!" he screamed.

And suddenly a blinding explosion ripped through the air. Anna's training kicked in, and she immediately shielded her face from the impact, feeling the heat wave wash over her. Debris flew everywhere, the van shook violently, and chaos ensued. As the smoke began to clear, Anna opened her eyes cautiously, her ears ringing from the blast.

Through the haze, she saw Greeves trying to get up, his ears bleeding from the explosion. Jefferson was on the ground, dazed but slowly regaining her senses. The man in the gray hoodie was nowhere to be seen.

The van was on fire now. The FBI agents in the front seat were groaning, clambering out of the wreck. Anna took this opportunity to make a rapid decision.

There, on the ground, a phone.

She hadn't spotted it before.

The screen cracked. The small device badly damaged.

The bad guy's phone?

She wasn't sure. Had Jefferson confiscated it? Also unsure. The hostile agent was clambering back to her feet, wincing and wiping blood from her mouth.

Anna snatched the phone off the ground. In the distance, the sound of approaching sirens.

Greeves lay unconscious behind her. She checked his vitals. Breathing. But stunned.

Then, pocketing the phone, she turned. "Hey! Hey! Stop!" Jefferson's voice shouted.

Anna ignored her, and instead broke into a jog, phone in her pocket, racing away from the scene. Two dead FBI agents. The man who'd likely killed them had blown himself up...

But amidst it all... the nagging realization.

Abdo Sahid was coming to the US. Maybe he was already here...

She scowled as she ran, her face forming a tapestry of furrowed lines. Jefferson's voice faded. The sound of the sirens continued to pierce the air above Mammoth Lakes.

She'd missed Abdo once before. How many young women and men had suffered because she'd failed the mission?

Was this redemption?

Was this fate or God's way of giving her a second chance?

She nodded to herself, certainty flooding through her as she continued to run, fleeing the scene, hand brushing against her pocket containing the damaged phone.

Another flash of an image. Her team had breached the compound. The teenage girl had begged Anna. Her large, brown eyes under a sweat-streaked brow. She'd pleaded with Anna. Please... please help me.

The same beeping. Faster, faster. Anna had tried to lunge in. She'd been dragged back. The last image: the girl's terrified face as she was left alone in a room to die.

Fatima. Anna had found out the girl's name only afterwards. A school girl kidnapped from her village by Sahid's men. In her head, Anna could still hear the girl's voice begging her for help.

And then the explosion.

How many other Fatimas were there?

Anna growled, sprinting now, indifferent to the ringing in her ears, or the pain lancing through her side from an old injury. She raced through the forest, back in the direction she'd come from.

Two dead agents.

Fatima dead.

And now Abdo was coming to her. And this time... this time, she wouldn't miss.

Chapter 5

To Anna, her RV was something of a sanctuary.

She sat in the driver's seat with her feet thrown up on the dash, overlooking a scenic view of the valley below: a labyrinth of greenery and craggy mountains surrounding a vast expanse of blue sky that was dotted with clouds. Her RV was built as a home but could manage speed as well thanks to the engine taken from a decommissioned tank—specifically, a Bradley Fighting Vehicle. The chassis was reinforced with layers of Kevlar, and the interior was equipped with a state-of-the-art surveillance system. It was the perfect hiding place for someone like Anna.

And now, on the FBI's radar, they would likely be breathing down her neck.

She glanced at the broken phone in her hand, stolen from the suicide bomber, a malformed lump of plastic and metal that looked like it could have been anything. But it was important, and she knew it.

She tightened her grip on the phone, feeling the rough edges dig into her palm. Her attention shifted to the laptop resting on her thighs. She lowered the phone, placing it on the seat next to her.

"Alright, then," she whispered to herself.

Anna's fingers flew over the laptop keyboard, the clattering sounding tinny in the cramped space of her RV. The screen glared back at her, pages flicking past as she searched tirelessly for any trace of "Fatima" in Yemen.

She tried "Faatimah," "Fatemah" – every conceivable variant that might lead to the news report of a woman's death from seven years ago. But the digital abyss returned nothing.

A scowl etched deeper into Anna's features. It wasn't just disappointment gnawing at her; there was a sharp worry that sliced through the fog of her exasperation. The FBI, with their relentless tendrils, were no doubt closing in on her. They'd want information, anything she knew about the man in the gray hood. And Anna had the sinking feeling they wouldn't ask nicely this time.

She clicked out of the browser and leaned back in her chair, rubbing at temples that throbbed with the beginning of a headache.

The silence of the RV hummed with tension, punctuated by the occasional distant car passing by outside.

The cursor blinked on Anna's laptop screen, a silent metronome marking the passing seconds as she sat motionless, her gaze locked on the broken phone that lay beside her. The arrival of Abdo Sahid to American soil was no longer a distant threat—it was an impending reality. Her fingers twitched involuntarily towards the device, its shattered screen a mosaic of possibilities.

She reached for it, the cracked plastic feeling cold and slightly jagged against her skin. Memories of the man in the gray hood flashed through her mind—the swift, merciless way he had wielded his blade against the unfortunate agents. Why had he been sent to kill the FBI? Or had they been sent to catch him? If so... he'd taken a permanent way out. Each fragment of glass from the phone's screen seemed to reflect a piece of the enigma that was Sahid.

"Violence as a message," she mused aloud, rolling the damaged phone between her palms. It was unlike Sahid to leave such a bloody trail; the man preferred shadows to daylight, manipulation over brute force. But this... this was personal, visceral. A shift in modus operandi that hinted at something more sinister.

Or something *bigger*. Where money was involved, Sahid would go to any lengths. He'd once killed his own father over a deal gone wrong.

Her thumb grazed over the exposed circuitry of the phone, where bits of metal and wire peeked out like the innards of some small woodland critter. If Sahid was escalating his methods to include public displays of violence, what did that say about his plans? What larger scheme could be worth exposing himself?

"Damn it," she whispered, frustration coiling in her chest.

The sharp rap of knuckles against metal jerked Anna from her thoughts. Her head snapped towards the door of the RV. She rose, muscles tensed, as another round of knocking hammered through the small space.

"Anna! It's me," a muffled voice called from outside, one she recognized instantly.

She exhaled slowly, grounding herself before pulling open the door to reveal the weathered face of Casper, his jaw set in that familiar stoic line. The corners of his eyes were crinkled, not from a smile but from days of strain and nights without proper rest. He wore sunglasses, like usual, his shaved head now topped with a baseball cap, the brim's shadow cast over his face.

He was handsome again—as she remembered him from back in the day. He'd shed some of the retirement pudge over the last couple months, and now she noted his masculine jawline, his strong shoulders. But there was no time to indulge in memories. Not when the FBI and a dangerous man like Abdo Sahid were breathing down their necks.

"Casper," Anna greeted him, stepping aside to allow him into the RV.

"Managed to give the feds the slip," he said, stepping inside without waiting for an invitation. "Beth's holed up in a motel, catching some Z's."

"You shouldn't be here, Cas," Anna warned, closing the door but unable to mask the relief in her voice. She studied him in the dim light, noting the way his hands never quite stilled – a soldier's habit. "Feds are looking for me."

"Neither should you," he pointed out, glancing around the cramped interior of her latest hideaway. "What's going down, Anna? Why're they sniffing our asses again?"

Anna hesitated. Casper had been out of the loop.

"Two dead feds. On our doorstep."

"Shit."

"Left-handed knife attack."

He glanced at her, quirked an eyebrow.

"Wasn't me."

"Just checking. So who?"

"Sahid," she uttered the name like a curse. "He's coming to town."

Casper's reaction was immediate; his posture stiffened, a hand instinctively brushing the place where a sidearm would normally rest. "Does he have his list? Checking it twice?"

"What?"

"Sorry. Bad joke. But you mean Abdo Sahid?" he demanded, uttering the name igniting a blaze in his eyes that Anna recognized all too well – the burning hatred for a shared enemy.

She nodded, watching as the anger settled into the hard lines of his face, etching years onto his features. They both knew what Sahid represented, the lives ruined in his wake.

Anna reached for the remnants of the shattered device on the small fold-out table, its screen a spider web of destruction. With a hesitant hand, she extended it towards Casper. "This might have something," she said, her voice low and edged with urgency.

Casper took the broken phone, turning it over in his calloused hands, the tactile memory of similar devices conjuring ghosts of operations past. He pressed the power button, but the screen remained lifeless, the silence from the device amplifying the tension in the confined space. "I can't crack this here," he finally admitted, looking up at Anna with a frown creasing his brow. "But I've got a contact. A guy who's good with tech."

"Good," Anna breathed out, relief momentarily easing the tightness in her chest. But as Casper pocketed the phone, her gaze drifted to the laptop screen still displaying a mosaic of search results, each a dead end. The frustration simmered within her again, a slow burn.

"We need to know what Sahid is planning," she said, more to herself than to Casper. Her fingers balled into fists atop the worn keyboard.

"Why?" Casper said simply.

She glanced at him. "How's that?"

"You're retired. We both are. He's..." Casper trailed off then shrugged. "He's their problem now."

Anna frowned, glancing at her old friend. "You don't know Sahid like I do," she said simply. "He's a dog. Needs to be put down."

"Aint your job anymore, though, is it?"

She continued to watch her old friend, still frowning.

Casper just shrugged at her from under his baseball cap. She began to pace the cramped interior of the RV, each step a metronome to their rising urgency. Casper watched her, leaning against the kitchenette counter, his normally aloof nature counteracting his initial reaction at the human trafficker's name.

She didn't reply at first, her mind still spinning. She tensed as she paced back and forth, wondering to herself... why?

She thought of her sister's family... The helicopter exploding. Now, Beth lived in pain. Anna knew that pain.

She'd never loved the same as Beth had—she'd never known the love of children. Of a husband... but she knew a different type. A camaraderie... A protectiveness.

They'd called her the Guardian. Anna Gabriel, an Angel of Death. She had always felt as if the work they did overseas made a difference. She'd dedicated her life to this belief. And now...

Now she wondered if she was just kidding herself.

Casper watched her, a mixture of admiration and sympathy in his eyes. "You can't stop asking questions," he said softly, almost gently. "You've always been like that."

He knew Anna's story well, the scars she bore from her years in the field. He'd seen her transform from a bright-eyed young recruit into a hardened warrior. But he also understood the toll it had taken on her.

"I saw the way you looked at that phone," he continued. "You won't let go until you know what Sahid's up to."

She paused, her eyes meeting his. "You're right," she said, her voice low and hoarse. "I can't let go. I need to know."

She knew she was chasing ghosts, trying to piece together a puzzle that had long since lost its pieces. But the name *Fatima* resounded in her mind. A child. Nothing more than a child, used as a play thing and discarded in an explosion.

Casper nodded in agreement. "Alright," he said. "Let's find out. What's your plan?"

Anna gave a brief smile, a hint of her old determination returning. "First, we figure out what's on this phone. Who's this guy you know?"

"Oh," he said with a smirk. "You've met him before. Good with computers. Bit of an asshole."

Anna tensed.

"Wait..."

"Waldo Strange the Third," Casper said, beaming now at the look on her face.

The conman had helped them rescue Beth three months before, but he'd also been the reason they'd found themselves knee-deep in shit in the first place. Waldo was self-diagnosed as something he called "ataraxic." He claimed he couldn't feel fear. In Anna's opinion, he was just a lippy asshole.

"He can help with this?"

"Yup. We got to know each other during stakeout. He's good with tech. And he's got the sorts of tools government types don't smile at. If we're looking local, he's our best bet."

Anna sighed, letting out a slow, irritated breath.

Before she could refuse, Casper slid into the front seat, beaming merrily. "I'll drive."

Chapter 6

The salon's doors creaked subtly as Anna and Casper slipped through, the dim lighting immediately swallowing their silhouettes. They moved with a deliberate quietness, shadows mingling with the smoke that hazed the air. The clinks of glass bottles and the low murmur of conversations were punctuated by the occasional harsh laugh, the soundscape of calculated risk and casual vice.

Anna's gaze was sharp beneath her hood, a hawk amongst pigeons, scanning the room with practiced efficiency. She kept her body language relaxed but every muscle was coiled, ready to spring into action at the slightest provocation. Casper, just a step behind her, mirrored her casual alertness, his hands tucked into the pockets of his worn leather jacket, eyes hidden behind dark shades despite the gloom.

They navigated through the maze of tables, sidestepping a waitress carrying a tray laden with empty glasses. The patrons paid them no mind, too engrossed in their own games of chance and cups of cheap liquor. The stench of stale beer mingled with the heavy smoke.

"You sure the asshole is here?" Anna muttered under her breath.

"Mhmm. Phone's pinging."

Anna just nodded, adjusting the hood concealing her features, and she scanned the late-night salon once more. Ostensibly a salon, but everyone in town knew it was a front for an off-hours gambling hall. The owner had brothers on the police force, and so law enforcement often looked the other way.

Anna, for her part, looked in every direction.

And then she paused, glaring at the table in the back of the room under a glowing, yellow light.

There, at a table set slightly apart from the rest, sat Waldo Strange. He was flanked by men also sitting at the table, holding hands of cards. These other men bore more ink on their skin than the pages of a novel, each tattoo a story of allegiance and threat. Their bulky forms seemed to meld together, a barrier of muscle and malice. Waldo's fingers danced upon his cards, his narrow eyes flicking about with a casual interest. Despite the jocular facade, there was a tension in his shoulders, a wariness that belied his apparent ease.

Casper's breath hitched almost imperceptibly as they spotted him; Anna felt it rather than heard it. A silent communication passed between them, a shared recognition of the quarry. They paused for a fraction of a second, recalibrating, before continuing their approach with measured strides.

With Waldo in their sights, the ambient noise of the salon seemed to recede, the focus narrowing. The click of chips and the shuffle of cards became the metronome to which they advanced, each step drawing them closer.

Anna's gaze sharpened, the hunter within on high alert. She watched as Waldo's fingers brushed his cards—a touch too deliberate—and then his ear, a seemingly innocuous gesture to the untrained eye. Across from him, a man with a viper tattoo coiling up his neck gave the briefest of nods, his hand shifting subtly.

Waldo's poker face was impenetrable, a mask of calm concentration. He was a seasoned player, well-versed in the art of deception, but Anna had seen it all before. She knew the signs, the subtle tells that gave away a cheater's hand. And right now, she was sure Waldo was up to something.

Casper hung back, his eyes darting from one player to another, searching for any signs of hostility or suspicion.

As they drew closer to the table, Anna could feel the buzz of anticipation in the air. Six players in total, all of them larger and more dangerous looking than the thin-framed Waldo. The men around the table were engrossed in their game, their minds solely focused on the cards in front of them. But there was an undertone of unease, a sense that something was off.

The man with the viper tattoo was particularly intimidating, his eyes raking over Anna and Casper as they approached. He didn't trust them, and Anna could sense it.

But Waldo didn't seem to notice the rising tension. He was too focused on the game, his fingers moving like lightning as he shuffled and dealt the cards.

"You're Big Blind," he said to the man at his left. This fellow was squat and beefy with hardly any neck.

The man grunted in acknowledgement, slapping down a stack of chips and turning his attention back to the game.

Casper and Anna continued to edge closer, their steps quiet and measured. They had seen this game before, the high stakes poker played in backrooms and shadows.

Waldo's scam partner was a shadowy figure, seated at the opposite end of the table. His eyes darted around, nervous and jumpy.

As the game continued, the tension in the room grew palpable. The players grew more and more agitated, their voices rising with each bet and bluff. Sweat beaded on their foreheads, and the air grew thick with the scent of cigar smoke and adrenaline.

One player, a man with a tribal tattoo snaking up his arm, slammed his fists on the table. "I'm all in," he exclaimed, shoving his chips forward.

Waldo eyed him coldly, his dollar-bill green eyes flashing. Waldo had the same lean figure she remembered, with extremely sharp cheekbones and a jawline beneath his mess of bedraggled hair as if he'd just got out of bed. His fingers drummed on the table. "Call," he said, swallowing hard.

The room fell silent as the other players weighed their options. The man with the tribal tattoo watched Waldo with a mixture of trepidation and scorn.

Suddenly, Waldo let out a low, throaty laugh.

The other players exchanged looks of irritation.

"Call," Waldo said. He shoved his chips towards the center of the table.

The big, beefy fellow with the tribal tattoo hesitated. He had a head like a misshapen potato, the two ears jutting out like protuberances.

Everyone watched, waiting for the players to reveal their cards, but Anna stepped forward before this happened, leaning down near Waldo and whispering in his ear.

"Time to go, Waldo," she murmured, her voice a velvet threat as she materialized beside his chair. Her sudden presence drew a flicker of surprise in his eyes, the only crack in his practiced veneer.

Waldo's pupils dilated, the horror seeping into the creases of his face as he met Anna's unwavering stare. "You?"

"Me," she replied. "Let's go."

"What the hell... no, hang on. This isn't—" His words faltered under her glacial gaze, fingers tightening around the edges of his cards.

"Shh," she hushed, a finger raised to her lips, her eyes never leaving his. With a tilt of her head, she glanced at the deck in his hands, then back to his eyes. It was a silent exchange, but her message was clear: I see your game.

He swallowed hard, a bead of sweat trickling down his temple as he tried to regain some semblance of composure. "I think you have the wrong impression," Waldo said, his voice edged with desperation, yet pitched low enough that only Anna could hear.

"Perhaps," Anna conceded softly, her expression unyielding. She leaned closer, her breath a whisper across the felt table. Her hand briefly touched her own ear, mirroring his earlier signal, and then fell away—a fleeting gesture unnoticed by the others, but a thunderous declaration to Waldo.

His mouth opened, then closed, any attempt to further plead his case dying in his throat. He knew the jig was up; Anna had seen through the charade.

"Who is this bitch?" the big, beefy man demanded, glaring between them.

"Time's up, Waldo. We're leaving," Anna said, her voice low but carrying the sharp edge of command.

The other players, their faces a tapestry of scars and ink, shifted restlessly in their seats. A collective discontent began to simmer as they picked up on the tension, their game interrupted by this interloper.

"Hey, sweetheart, why don't you let the men play?" grumbled the burly player with the tribal tattoo from the end of the table. He had arms like steel cables and eyes that held a glint of malice.

His comment hung in the air, laced with a venomous tone that suggested he was not used to being ignored.

"Your concern is touching," Anna replied, her voice calm and even, giving nothing away. Her gaze didn't waver from Waldo's pale face, but she was acutely aware of the hulking presence trying to unnerve her.

"Back off, bitch," snapped the beefy man, pointing a finger at her. "Or I'll have to spank you."

The tension crackled between the clustered tables as Casper moved, a silent shadow detaching from the wallpapered obscurity of the salon's interior. His eyes, dark and steady, locked onto the beefy guy whose remarks slithered like oil on water. "You'll shut your mouth now," Casper said, his voice a low rumble, each syllable dropped like a stone in still waters.

A smirk curled the edges of the big man's lips, his head tilting back to appraise Casper with an air of mockery that hung thick in the smoky air. "Or what? You gonna make me, pretty boy?"

Casper's jaw tightened, the muscles flexing beneath the skin with restrained anger, his stance widening ever so slightly—a subtle signal of his readiness to act. But before he could reply, the beefy player turned back to Anna, his hand shooting out in a vulgar swipe that connected sharply with her backside.

The sound—a vile and disrespectful crack—ricocheted around the room, punctuating the silence with its audacity. The line, invisible yet palpably present in moments prior, was now crossed, the boundaries of decency shattered.

Casper's retreat was almost imperceptible, a mere shifting of weight to his back foot, as he yielded the floor to Anna. The air crackled with tension, the salon's usual cacophony dimming into a suspenseful hush. Casper sighed.

The beefy man chuckled, noticing Casper's retreat. "Ha. See? You won't do shit."

Casper just shook his head. "Nah. I just don't wanna get in the way when she kicks your ass. Shit, man. You've done it now."

"Apologize," Anna's voice cut through the quiet, deceptively serene, her eyes never leaving the face of the man who had touched her. The command was not loud but carried the weight of absolute expectation; it was not a request.

The beefy guy scoffed, his face contorting into an ugly sneer as he wound up for another strike, emboldened by the gallery of onlookers. But as his hand arced through the air towards Anna, time seemed to dilate. She sidestepped with the fluid grace of a dancer, her expression unchanging, her gaze cold and sharp.

As his palm neared its intended target, Anna's hand shot out—a blur of motion—seizing his wrist in an ironclad grip. The snap of bone was crisp, definitive, reverberating through the room like a gunshot. His howl sliced the silence, a pained animal noise that had him crumpling to his knees.

The salon erupted into murmurs and gasps, patrons recoiling from the display of swift retribution. Anna stood above the groaning man, her poise unshaken.

The sudden chorus of curses heralded new challengers; two goons, muscles rippling under ink-stained skin, detached themselves from the shadowy corner at the back of the room.

Anna's posture was relaxed, but her mind raced, calculating distances and trajectories. Her eyes flickered between the advancing threats, taking stock of their reach and momentum. The first one, larger and presumably slower, raised a ham-sized fist, telegraphing his intent. The second, wiry and snarling, moved to flank her.

But Anna was an avalanche waiting to happen. She pivoted on the ball of her foot, meeting the larger man's attack with an economy of motion. Her palm struck the inside of his elbow, redirecting the energy of his punch into empty space. With her other hand, she delivered a sharp jab to his throat, causing instant spasms as airways constricted—a temporary but debilitating setback.

The wiry one lunged, thinking to catch her off balance, but Anna was already shifting her stance. She dropped low, her leg sweeping out in a wide arc, catching his ankles and sending him crashing onto the poker table, which groaned and splintered under his weight.

Rising fluidly, Anna didn't pause to admire her handiwork. Instead, she stepped towards the larger goon who was still gasping for breath, clutching at his throat. A precise chop to the side of his neck, targeting the bundle of nerves she knew would be there, sent him tumbling down like a felled tree.

In moments, both men lay incapacitated on the floor, the threat they posed neutralized.

The chilling click of hammers being cocked sliced through the thick tension in the air. Anna pivoted on her heel, her gaze locking onto two more poker players as they pushed back their chairs and rose. The metallic glint of their guns was unmistakable, even in the dimly lit room.

Anna's body reacted faster than thought. She lunged forward, closing the gap between them with startling speed. The first gunman barely had time to level his weapon before Anna was upon him. She twisted his arm upward, redirecting the barrel towards the ceiling just as it expelled a thunderous shot that rained plaster down upon them.

The second man's finger twitched towards his trigger, but Anna was already in motion. A swift kick to his wrist sent the gun skittering across the floor. She followed up with a knee to his abdomen, forcing the air from his lungs in a pained grunt. As he doubled over, she grabbed the back of his head, slamming it onto the edge of the table with a crack that echoed the finality of a judge's gavel.

Both threats were neutralized, the guns now nothing more than expensive paperweights on the grimy floor.

Casper was leaning against the back wall, sipping a beer that had been left by one of the gunmen.

Anna rolled her eyes and flashed him the middle finger. He smirked.

The cacophony of the brawl had faded into a ringing silence, punctuated only by the ragged breaths of the fallen. Anna's gaze landed on Waldo Strange, his wiry frame hunched over the table as if in prayer.

But piety wasn't at play here; his hands were a blur, rifling through the scattered bills with the desperation of a starving man at a feast. The chaos had become his smokescreen, a chance to pocket the illicit earnings under the guise of confusion.

"Really, Waldo?" Anna's voice sliced through the quiet. He flinched, his head snapping up to meet her eyes.

Across the room, the door crashed open against the wall with a violent thud. Waldo's scam partner, a twitchy fellow with an eye always on the exit, had bolted. His chair toppled backward, clattering to the floor as he made a mad dash, his silhouette a fleeting shadow against the dim light from the street outside. Panic lent wings to his feet.

Anna watched him flee. She didn't move to chase; she was the spider now, and Waldo was caught in her web.

Grasping the fabric of Waldo's shirt tightly, Anna's fingers clenched around his collar with unyielding intent. His attempts at charm dissolved against the steel of her resolve, his quips fading into the tense air as if they had never been uttered.

"Enough," she said, voice low and steady. Her eyes, two flints ready to spark a wildfire, locked onto his with a message that brokered no argument. The humor drained from Waldo's face.

Without waiting for his surrender, she tugged sharply on his collar, propelling him towards the back door. The sound of their hurried footsteps echoed in the hush that followed the fight.

Casper joined them.

"Hang on, ack! I can't breathe!" Waldo protested, kicking and shoving at Anna.

"Stop," she said simply.

"No means no!" he quipped. "Let me go! Dammit, Anna—let me go!"

She shoved him out the back door, into the alley. Waldo was massaging his throat, staring at her with a look of irritation. But the professional wiseass couldn't keep quiet. "What the hell was that? I'm working!"

Casper slammed the door shut behind them, blocking it with one of the large dumpsters, rolling it in place to wedge against the metal handle. A few seconds later, the door creaked, and voices shouted. More threats were trying to emerge into the alley.

Anna quickly glanced around the cramped space, and she nodded towards a ladder in the back. Casper hoisted Waldo on one side while Anna grabbed his other.

"Really, I'm flattered," Waldo said. "But I'm not into threesomes. Unless you've got another pretty friend. How's your sister, doing, Anna?" He squawked as she shoved him towards the ladder.

"Climb, asshole!"

He sighed, but then, at the sound of voices shouting around the front of the establishment now, he took this as his cue to hasten up onto the roof. Anna and Casper hastily followed.

Once they reached the roof, they all took a moment to catch their breath. The twitchy scam partner was nowhere in sight, having managed to escape through an unguarded alleyway. Waldo rubbed his neck and glowered at Anna, his face a mask of frustration.

"So," she said, crossing her arms, "I take it you weren't planning on sharing your winnings with your partner there?"

Waldo smirked nervously, "You always had a way with words."

Casper looked between them, calmly appraising the situation. "Well, looks like you didn't learn your lessons before. And I quote, *I swear, I'll live an honest life from now on.*"

"I didn't know it was going to turn into a full-blown shootout," Waldo defended.

Anna rolled her eyes. "Oh, please."

Waldo sighed, rubbing his eyes. "Okay, so let's say I didn't fully anticipate the fireworks. But they were just a few of my regulars, and they're always eager to play. I never intended to cheat them out of their money; it was just a bit of harmless fun."

Anna looked at him skeptically. "Move!" She gave him another shove and the three of them hastened towards a stairwell centering the roof.

They took the stairs two at a time and emerged in a side street where they'd parked.

"What's this about?" Waldo demanded. "I paid my debt—shit, stop shoving me!"

"We need your help," Casper said simply.

"Helluva way to ask a fellow. Ever tried please and thank you?"

"Please?" Casper said.

"Hell no. Let me go."

"Thank you," Anna said, shoving the con man into the RV. Casper followed, and Anna hastened around the front, slipping into the driver's seat. Waldo—busy trying to climb out the bathroom window—yelped as Casper dragged him back into the RV.

"Sit," Casper commanded. "Please," he added. And then he tripped Waldo, sending him clattering to the floor.

Anna backed the RV out of the parking lot, her eyes darting between the rearview mirror and the main road. Casper helped Waldo to his feet, and the two men exchanged tense glances.

"You know, you're not making this easy, Strange," Casper said, his voice low and threatening.

"I was having a grand old time back there. Literally. You owe me a grand."

Anna snorted, her fingers tightening around the steering wheel. "You owe us," she said simply.

"I paid that debt!" he declared.

"Not by my count," Anna retorted.

"That business with Beth's family… that's tragic," Waldo said, swallowing. "Truly. But I didn't do shit." He stared at her, wide-eyed in the mirror as she navigated away from the salon.

"We need you to get into a phone," Casper said simply. "And we need you to do it tonight."

"Do I have a choice."

"Yes."

"Then the answer is no."

"The other option is I break your fingers."

Waldo sighed, rolling his eyes and subtly shifting his posture so he was sitting on his hands where Casper couldn't reach his fingers. "Fine," he muttered. "But I'm complaining to HR."

Chapter 7

"Don't rough him up too bad," Casper's voice came from the front seat after they'd pulled to a halt outside Waldo's apartment.

Anna glanced back towards her RV, frowned, but flashed a thumbs up. Then she followed after their reluctant associate. Waldo hastened up a set of metal stairs towards the second floor of a duplex. He reached the door, keyed a card, entered a passcode and then undid a small strip of tape under the door before easing it open.

"Me casa es me casa," he called over his shoulder.

"Not sure that's how the expression goes," she muttered.

"I know what I said."

She followed up the stairs and reached the door. Waldo looked like he was considering if he ought to slam it in her face. In the end, he must've spotted the look in her eye, because he decided against it.

She followed him, her boots thumping softly on the worn carpet as they ascended a narrow staircase littered with small electronic parts that hinted at the kind of dangerous tinkering Waldo was apparently familiar with. The steps creaked under their weight, each groan a testament to the countless times Waldo must have run up and down in bouts of frenzied inspiration or paranoia.

The top of the stairs opened into a chaotic living space where disorder was clearly the norm. Amongst the clutter, expensive gadgets and devices lay carelessly across a large wooden table that served as the centerpiece of Waldo's apartment. Loose wires formed a nest around a soldering iron, while high-end camera lenses sat adjacent to what looked suspiciously like rare antique coins. It was a cornucopia of valuables that no ordinary salary could account for—each item a silent accusation of Waldo's extracurricular activities.

"Sorry about the mess," he said with a nonchalant wave of his hand, not seeming sorry at all. "I've been busy with projects."

"It's fine," Anna muttered, though she couldn't help but raise an eyebrow at the opulent disarray. She knew better than to question him outright; Waldo's business was his own, as long as he delivered on hers. She spotted a pile of pearl necklaces by the window, and an old painting that looked suspiciously like an original.

"Let's get to work then," Waldo said, his tone shifting to one of reluctant resignation as he motioned for her to follow him deeper into his lair.

Anna's shadow trailed behind her as she stepped into the back room, a cramped space that smelled of solder and burnt circuits. Waldo flicked on a desk lamp, its harsh light cutting through the dimness to spotlight an organized chaos of tools laid out with precision on a worn table. His fingers danced over the array of screwdrivers, tweezers, and magnifying glasses before selecting a tiny Torx bit.

She leaned against the doorframe, arms folded, watching as Waldo cradled the charred remains of the phone like a surgeon preparing for a delicate procedure.

With deft fingers, he coaxed the screws from their melted housing, setting them aside with a soft clink onto the metal tray. The back cover came off with a gentle pry, revealing the guts of the phone—its internal components warped by heat.

"Seen better days," Waldo muttered, more to himself than to Anna. "Same could be said for you, you know," he added, glancing up at her. "Wouldn't kill you to make an effort, would it?"

"I don't take fashion advice from a conman," she replied.

"No... looks like you take it from a hobo. Just kidding!" he added with a yelp as she took a step towards him, but she was simply moving closer to examine the device.

"Get on with it," she said.

He nodded and reached for a pair of angled tweezers and a small, flat tool designed to navigate the circuitry without causing further damage. With each component he disconnected, Anna's anticipation grew.

She observed how his brow furrowed, his tongue peeking out in concentration as he delicately separated the hard drive from its plastic tomb.

"Almost there," he said, finally breaking the silence. The hard drive, though battered, sat unscathed in Waldo's palm.

Waldo's hands, steady as a surgeon's, ushered the hard drive into the waiting card reader with a gentle click. The device was nondescript, a mere conduit to the charred silicon. He connected it to his computer, the LED light blinking to life—a heartbeat in the dimly lit back room.

Anna leaned closer, her breath held in quiet suspense, eyes locked on the screen as it flickered, acknowledging the new connection. Every whir and hum from Waldo's machine punctuated the silence that stretched between them, thick with expectation. Her fingers curled into the fabric of her jeans, knuckles white, as the usual start-up chime of the computer seemed to announce the precipice of discovery.

The desktop came alive, an array of icons and shortcuts scattered across the digital landscape. Waldo navigated through them with practiced ease. A window popped open, revealing file directories in stark, monochrome text—most were corrupted, their names now gibberish, casualties of the fire that had ravaged the phone.

"Come on," Waldo whispered. His cursor hovered. Files opened and closed in rapid succession, a blur of images and broken code before Anna's eyes until—

"Here," Waldo said, his voice a low growl of triumph. A single, uncorrupted message materialized on the screen, its contents stark against the white background. An address, no more than a string of numbers and a name, but it was enough to send a jolt through Anna's veins.

Waldo entered the address in the web search engine, and an image appeared instantly, along with a five star review bar. "Well, well," Waldo murmured. "Chateau Royale."

Anna stared at the image of a large casino in Las Vegas, its facade notorious even in the pixelated image accompanying the text.

A breadcrumb on a trail that led to the heart of the neon desert.

Anna leaned closer to the monitor, the facade of the casino burning into her retinas. "Who owns this casino?"

Waldo's fingers paused their dance over the keyboard, and he glanced up at Anna, a glimmer of—was it envy?—flashing across his eyes. "No one good," he said, the corners of his mouth tilting upwards ever so slightly. "That much is a given in this industry. You've never heard of Chateau Royale?"

"No."

"Damn. Don't teach you killing machines any culture, do they?"

"Waldo. What is this place?"

Waldo leaned back, looking happy that he knew something she didn't. In the light of the room, she was struck at just how trim he was. His features were gaunt, and his cheekbones stood out against his skin. The low body fat percentage suggested a man who didn't eat much or worked out plenty. He had a runner's physique.

Now, Waldo was shaking his head, side to side, "I... I really am sorry about Beth... and all that. Her family."

"Could still be alive."

"Oh. Umm. You heard something?"

"Nothing. You?"

"No," he said hastily, wagging a finger over his heart. "I swear. Nothing."

"So Chateau Royale," she interjected, tapping a finger against the screen. "Who owns it?"

"The owner's a ghost in high society, whispers in the wind, but anyone who's anyone knows you don't cross paths with them unless you're looking for trouble. Mob connections and the sort. Las Vegas," Waldo murmured, almost to himself, as he leaned back in his chair. It creaked under his weight, echoing in the cluttered space. His gaze drifted past the mountain of tech gadgets on his desk, past the walls of his apartment, to lands paved with neon dreams.

He chuckled, the sound tinged with a longing that seemed to reach out from him and touch the very edges of the dusty room.

"Adventure, excitement... Las Vegas thrives on it like nowhere else." Waldo met Anna's eyes then, and she could see it—the itch for escapism, the lure of the unknown that beckoned him towards the siren call of the desert city.

Anna squared her shoulders and turned away from the screen, where a series of cryptic files still flickered in a digital dance. "I have to go," she stated, the words falling between them with the weight of inevitability.

Waldo perked up, his head tilting like an intrigued bird. The glow from the monitors picked out the gleam in his eyes, a spark that hadn't been there moments before. He stood up swiftly, knocking over a small pile of screwdrivers which clattered to the floor, unheeded. "Hey, I know that place inside out. The back alleys, the high-roller suites. You shouldn't go alone." His voice carried an earnestness that, under any other circumstances, might have sounded endearing.

"Alone is exactly how I should go," Anna countered without missing a beat.

"Come on, Anna." He motioned around the cluttered room that spoke volumes of his life, "I can be useful," he pleaded, stepping closer.

She caught the hint of desperation in his stance, the subtle shift from confident to hopeful. It was a vulnerability she rarely saw in him, but she couldn't afford the luxury of sentimentality. Her gaze remained fixed, unwavering as she responded. "Las Vegas is my play, and I run a solo game."

"Anna—"

"No, Waldo," she cut him off, her tone final. "This isn't about what you need. You said it yourself; no one good owns that casino. Why meddle? Besides."

"What? Don't you trust me?"

"Not a lick."

"Hurtful. Still, let me earn your trust! I can do that! Scout's honor!"

She shook her head, taking a photo of the address on her own phone, then hastening towards the door.

Anna's hand had just touched the doorknob when she heard the distinct shuffling of Waldo behind her. She turned, frowning as she caught sight of him stuffing a compact toolkit into his jacket and slipping on a pair of worn leather boots.

"Seriously?" she said, exasperation lacing her words. "I thought we settled this."

"Settled? Maybe for you," he retorted, brushing past her. His voice carried a hint of stubbornness that Anna knew all too well. "But I never signed off on any agreement."

Anna followed him down the staircase, her eyes narrowing. It was like trying to shake a particularly tenacious dog off a bone. Waldo had always been persistent, but this was bordering on obstinate intrusion. His footsteps echoed through the otherwise quiet building.

"Where do you think you're going?" Anna pressed, catching up to him at the building's entrance.

"Vegas, baby," he replied without breaking stride. "You don't have to like it, but you might need me. Besides, Casper likes having me around."

The RV came into view, a hulking silhouette against the fading light. Casper, ever the vigilant sentinel, sat perched on the driver's seat, his gaze shifting from the rearview mirror to the two figures approaching.

"Look, Waldo," Anna said, stopping short of the vehicle, "I'm not taking you to Vegas."

He glared at her. "Because of you, I lost a score tonight. Some bad guys gonna be stopping by my place. You owe me this much."

"I don't owe you shit. If not for you, my baby sister wouldn't be grieving."

"I didn't intend any of that. You're blaming me, but it's the albino's fault."

Anna knew he was telling the truth, in a way. Waldo had been careless, but not malicious. And he did have his uses. She'd just seen him running a con at a poker table. He might be useful in a place like Vegas. Especially where Abdo Sahid was concerned.

She sighed. She knocked on the window.

"You like this guy?" she asked.

Casper blinked behind his sunglasses. "How's that?"

"Waldo wants to come with."

"Oh? Where the hell we going?"

"Vegas. Just a day trip."

"I can't," Casper said with a shrug.

Anna blinked.

"Your sister paid me, not you. I gotta stick by Beth."

Anna paused only briefly. The sting of losing her most reliable confidant flared through her, but just as quickly she nodded.

She saw the sense in this. "Fair." Besides, she liked the idea of Casper keeping an eye on Beth.

"But yeah. I like him. He's annoying, but he's amusing."

"That's what I'm talking about!" Waldo called from behind Anna.

She sighed.

Casper shrugged. "Drop me off at the motel?"

"Sure. But don't tell Beth what I'm doing."

"Wouldn't dream of it."

Chapter 8

In the shadowed confines of the cramped truck cabin, Dalton perched on the edge of a threadbare front seat, his eyes unblinking as they bore into the grainy footage flickering across the monitor before him above the dashboard. The screen's dim glow cast ghostly patterns on his sharp features, while the rest of his face was etched in darkness.

On the monitor, the new girl, Jacinth's image trembled slightly, the camera feed juddering with the motion of the truck. Her face, illuminated by the harsh overhead light within her confined space, was marred with streaks of tears that glistened against her pale skin. Her chest rose and fell rapidly, betraying her terror even as she tried to steel herself against it.

He'd been there when they'd dragged away the two feds. The woman had made a break for it. Nearly escaped. But she'd been hunted down, just like her partner.

Dalton felt a strange twinge in his chest, an unexpected blend of pity and something darker, more primal. It stirred within him as he took in the delicate curve of her jaw, the way her hair clung to her damp forehead. He knew to keep his emotions barricaded when it came to the merchandise—empathy was a luxury he couldn't afford in this line of work—but Jacinth's vulnerability chipped away at his resolve.

"Dammit," he muttered under his breath, chastising himself for the unwelcome surge of protectiveness that accompanied his begrudging admiration. He shouldn't be affected by her beauty or her plight; she was just another job. Yet as her eyes, wide and pleading, seemed to look right through the camera lens and into his soul, Dalton felt the weight of a silent plea that he couldn't ignore.

The truck shuddered to a halt, its heavy brakes groaning under the strain. As Dalton peered through the front windshield, his gaze was momentarily ensnared by the spectacle that unfurled before him. Las Vegas loomed in the distance like a mirage made of phosphorescence and steel, its luminescent glow pulsating against the dark curtain of night. The city buzzed with an electric frenzy, each flickering sign and streaming headlight a testament to life lived out loud.

He glanced back at the monitor, where Jacinth's image flickered in bleak contrast. Where the city promised indulgence, the back of the truck offered nothing but shadows and despair.

"Maybe just a few words," Dalton found himself thinking, the idea sneaking into his consciousness despite his better judgment. "Just to let her know she's not alone." He sought justification in the thought, a flimsy excuse to sate the gnawing guilt that clawed at him. His fingers twitched involuntarily, betraying his urge to comfort her.

"Damn it, Dalton," he scolded himself silently. "She's cargo, not a damsel in distress." Yet her tear-streaked face haunted him, challenging his steadfast detachment. "But what harm could it do? Maybe it'll even calm her down, make her more... compliant." Maybe she'd reward him... maybe he could sample the goods.

He wrestled with the notion, his mind a battleground of duty and arousal. The rules were clear, etched into his role like commandments: Do not engage. Keep it professional. No personal involvement. And yet, as he watched her desperate eyes scour the confines of her prison, Dalton's resolve began to waver.

He rationalized further, his thoughts spiraling. "It's not like I'm breaking her or anything. Just...human connection. That's all."

On the monitor, Jacinth shifted uncomfortably, her chains clinking softly in the silence. Despite everything, despite the cold facade he'd built over years in this grim trade, Dalton felt himself inching towards a decision he knew could unravel with the slightest tug—a decision driven not by protocol, but by something much more dangerous.

As he came to a full halt in the truck stop, Dalton's hand pressed against the cold metal of the door, a hollow *clunk* reverberating as he pushed it open. The night air rushed in to fill the void left by the truck's stagnant interior, carrying with it the distant pulse of Las Vegas life.

The tension hung palpable in the desert chill, a silent observer to the turmoil brewing within Dalton. Each stride carried him closer to the truck's rear, his shadow stretching long and distorted across the ground, a dark companion to his troubled thoughts. "Just a few words," he murmured to himself, the sound swallowed by the vastness around them.

Reaching the back of the truck, Dalton's hands met resistance as they groped for the handle—his fingers wrapping around the cold, unyielding latch. He tugged, expecting compliance, but the door remained steadfast. His brow furrowed, frustration flaring like a match strike in the dark.

"Come on," he growled under his breath, muscles tensing as he exerted more force. The door held firm, mocking his efforts with its stubborn silence. Dalton's heart pounded against his ribcage, each throb echoing the growing urgency that knotted his stomach.

"Damn thing," he muttered, yanking harder, the veins in his forearms standing out in stark relief against his skin.

With one final, desperate pull, Dalton threw his entire weight into the effort, his face set in grim determination.

The door burst open. It struck him with force, sending him staggering backward into the gritty asphalt stage of the truck's shadow. His breath hitched, a sharp gasp painting the night air white as his back collided with the unforgiving ground. Pain radiated from his shoulder where the metal edge had hit.

Dazed, Dalton blinked against the glaring overhead lights that now seemed to mock his disorientation.

"Jacinth," he groaned, the name coming out as a pained whisper, more accusation than call.

The sight within the truck horrified him.

The chains dangled empty, their ends swaying slightly. Dalton's heart lurched, pounding a frenetic rhythm against his chest as his gaze darted around the vacant space.

"How?" The word fell flat.

And then a blur of movement as she jumped past him, hurtling from inside the dark truck, out onto the street.

He lunged... missed.

She scampered past.

Regaining his balance, Dalton's gaze snapped toward the open expanse beyond the truck. There, Jacinth's silhouette flickered in the stark light of a distant streetlamp. Her figure was a blur of desperation as she seized her fleeting chance at freedom.

"Stop!" His voice rang out, the command sharp and instinctive, but it was swallowed by the void between them. Dalton watched in horror.

With each pound of her feet against the unforgiving pavement, the gap widened, and Dalton felt the vice of panic tighten around his chest. She was getting away, and with her, his reputation, his security, everything he'd worked for was sprinting into the night.

Without conscious thought, his hand flew to the sidearm holstered at his hip. Fingers that had caressed the grip countless times now fumbled with the clasp, his movements erratic and clumsy. The metallic click of the release seemed unnaturally loud, echoing ominously in the tense silence.

Dalton drew the weapon, his arm extending with a tremor. Sweat beaded on his brow, despite the chill in the air, and his breath came in short gasps, fogging the air before him.

He squinted, aiming down the barrel, trying to steady his aim despite the cocktail of adrenaline coursing through him. His finger hovered over the trigger.

"Dammit," he whispered to the fleeing figure, "just stop."

The night held its breath, waiting for the crack of gunfire to shatter the stillness.

Dalton's eyes widened in disbelief as Jacinth's silhouette darted between the blinding headlights of oncoming traffic. The screech of tires and horns filled the air as she narrowly dodged a sedan that swerved violently to avoid her, its driver laying on the horn.

"Damn it!" Dalton spat out the words as she vaulted a metal barrier.

The guard's muscles ached to sprint, to give chase, but his feet betrayed him, rooted to the gravel-strewn ground as if cast in concrete. What if a witness spotted him. Las Vegas had cops. A lot of them. His pulse hammered in his ears, a rhythmic reminder of the stakes at play. A surge of heat flushed his face at the thought of facing his superiors empty-handed; the humiliation of failure was a bitter pill, more toxic than any reprimand.

"Backup," the word lingered on his tongue, a lifeline beckoning with the promise of reinforcement.

"Control," his voice crackled over the radio, "I need—" The transmission cut short, the rest of his plea swallowed by the lump forming in his throat. Dalton's finger lingered on the call button, a silent acknowledgment of his own dread. No... no, if he told them what had happened, it was his skin on the line.

He ended the call.

With a swift movement, he tucked his weapon into the back of his waistband, hidden beneath the hem of his jacket.

He rounded the corner, eyes scanning the darkened alleyways for any sign of movement. A clang echoed down the street—a trash can overturned in haste, perhaps? He veered toward the sound, each stride fueled by a potent cocktail of desperation and terror.

His breath came in ragged gasps, the cool night air searing his lungs.

He had to find her... And fast.

Chapter 9

The desert sun cast a golden hue over the strip as the RV rumbled into Las Vegas, the city's neon beginning to flicker against the twilight. Waldo's face was plastered to the window, eyes wide with child-like wonder, his breath fogging up the glass as they passed one glitzy establishment after another.

"Look at that!" he exclaimed, pointing at the towering fountains that danced in synchrony with the pulsing lights.

"Easy, Waldo," Anna said, her hands steady on the wheel. "Remember why we're here."

Waldo turned toward her, the buzz of excitement still evident in his lean frame as he bounced lightly in his seat. "Sure, sure. But it's Vegas!"

Anna pulled into a quieter side street and parked the RV with practiced ease. She turned off the engine and swiveled her chair to face Waldo, her expression serious and commanding.

"Listen," she started, holding his gaze to ensure she had his full attention. "We can't afford any slip-ups."

He nodded, but his eyes were glued to the building ahead of them.

The Chateau Royale rose from the desert like a mirage, its gilded façade reflecting the dying sunlight in a spectacle of opulence that rivaled the setting sun. Towering fountains danced at the entrance, choreographed jets of water sparkling against the darkening sky. Marble statues peered down from their lofty perches, silent sentinels to the secrets held within the casino's cavernous halls.

"Wow," Waldo breathed out, his face pressed against the RV's passenger window, eyes wide with awe.

"Keep it together, Waldo," Anna murmured absently, her gaze fixed on the grand scene. She couldn't afford to get lost in the splendor; every glimmering light was a potential hiding spot for danger, every polished surface a mirror that could reveal too much.

She unhooked the walkie-talkie from her belt and handed it to him, her movements precise and deliberate. "Waldo, I need you here."

His excitement was replaced by a flicker of confusion. "Here?"

"Exactly here, in the RV," she clarified, her tone leaving no room for debate. "You're my eyes and ears on the outside. If anyone so much as looks at this vehicle, I want to know about it immediately."

"Sure, but—" His protest died under her steady gaze.

"Check the doors, keep the radio on, and stay alert," she instructed, her fingers tapping the dashboard rhythmically, underscoring the gravity of his task. "This isn't just another pit stop. See if anyone follows me out. Take pictures of anyone entering or leaving this place. Got it?"

He grabbed the radio and tested the button. He stared longingly at the casino. "I... I feel like I could do better from the inside."

"Waldo... I need to rely on you here. Do what I say, got it?"

Before he could protest further, Anna stepped out of the RV into the balmy evening air, the scent of desert flowers tempting her to relax. But her body remained tense.

As the door shut behind her, sealing Waldo inside their makeshift command center, Anna allowed herself a moment to take in the grandeur of Chateau Royale once more. But rather than indulging in its beauty, she assessed its weaknesses, its potential threats. Her mission was clear, and in the depths of Las Vegas' glittering jewel, she would find what she came for. Abdo Sahid's hitman had kept this address in his phone. The only question was why?

The casino loomed before her, a titan of temptation, but her stride was unwavering as she moved past rows of vehicles that gleamed under the canopy lights.

Luxury cars — Bentleys, Lamborghinis, even a rare Aston Martin — lined the VIP section, their polished chrome and sleek lines declaring the wealth that flowed as freely as the drinks inside. Valets in crisp uniforms scurried between them, escorting guests from shiny doorsteps to the sheltered opulence of Chateau Royale's main entrance. Anna took note of each face, every movement, her senses heightened. She passed a couple laughing, the woman's diamonds catching the light with a sparkle.

Infiltrate, observe, expose — the mantra that beat in time with her footsteps as she approached the grand doors of the casino.

The sweep of violins and the gentle harp cascaded through the grand foyer as Anna crossed the threshold into Chateau Royale's cavernous embrace. Above her, crystal chandeliers poured golden light over marble floors that gleamed like still waters at dawn. The walls were adorned with tapestries and paintings that could have been plucked from the halls of European palaces. She inhaled deeply, the scent of money and perfume mingling with the subtle undertones of aged wood. This casino wasn't like any other she'd heard of. More country lodge than neon spectacle. Though both facets existed in tandem, the closer she looked.

She moved with a calm assertiveness, her eyes drinking in every detail—the plush velvet ropes cordoning off private areas, the discreetly placed security cameras, and the soft clinking of chips that punctuated the music's lilt. It was all designed to seduce and disarm, but Anna's mind worked, cataloging vulnerabilities, memorizing escape routes.

"Welcome to Chateau Royale," a voice cut through the orchestrated hum. A young woman in a red suit, crisp and impeccably tailored, approached with a practiced smile. Her badge read 'Claire.'

"Good evening. Do you have a reservation with us?" Claire's tone was polite, yet it carried an undercurrent of scrutiny. She appraised Anna with a glance that seemed to take in every inch of her appearance, searching for telltale signs of status.

Anna met her gaze evenly. She wore a simple leather jacket and running slacks. Hardly the same get-up as the rest of the clientele. "Not yet," she replied smoothly.

Claire's smile didn't waver, but her eyes narrowed just a fraction—a silent acknowledgment of the dance they were both performing. "Very well," she said. "If you'll follow me, I can assist you with your accommodations." Her heels clicked against the marble, echoing the rhythm of the classical masterpiece that swirled around them, as she led Anna deeper into the heart of Chateau Royale. "How many nights would you like to stay?"

Claire's poised fingers hovered above the polished surface of her tablet, awaiting Anna's response.

"Actually, I'm looking for someone who might already be staying here," Anna said, feigning a relaxed smile as she leaned against the mahogany concierge desk. "Abdo Sahid?"

The name seemed to snag in the air between them, and Claire's professional facade faltered for a split second before she regained her composure. Her eyes, sharp as cut diamonds, flicked up to Anna's, searching for intent. "Do you have his room number?" she asked, her voice betraying a hint of caution, the words deliberately slow.

"No," Anna replied, shaking her head subtly as she watched Claire's expression, a poker face honed by countless similar inquiries. "I was hoping you could help me locate him."

Claire tapped at her tablet, her brows knitting together ever so slightly. "One moment, please." She turned slightly away, affording Anna the opportunity she needed.

With a glance spared toward the opulent foyer—a dizzying array of gilded frames and plush velvet—Anna took advantage of the diversion. She sidled back from the counter, her footsteps silent on the carpet that swallowed sound as effectively as it did fortunes. As Claire's attention remained fixed on the screen, Anna melded into the throng of guests, a shadow among the light and laughter.

Anna weaved through the clusters of gambling tables and slot machines, her eyes darting from one face to another. The clinking of chips and the melodic chimes of the slots called to unwitting victims.

She scrutinized the throngs of people, a predator hunting amidst the bright lights. Couples laughed with feigned nonchalance, business men in tailored suits nursed drinks with a calculated air of indifference, and waitresses floated between them, offering poison in crystal flutes. But none of these held Anna's interest.

Her attention snagged on a trio near the bar, where the dim lighting cast long shadows over the patrons. Two women leaned into a man whose laughter boomed louder than the ambient music. His suit was expensive, his tie loose, his demeanor that of a man drowning in spirits and the illusion of luck. But it was the women who drew Anna's focus. Their dresses were tight and short, cut to advertise the flesh beneath, and their smiles—too wide, too fixed—were telltale masks of feigned affection.

One woman tossed her hair, dyed a brassy blonde, her arm snaking around the man's shoulder. Her movements were practiced, sensual yet devoid of genuine interest. The other, with raven-black tresses, laughed at something inaudible, her hand resting possessively on the man's thigh. Their posture, their painted faces, their eyes scanning the room even as they fawned over the drunkard—all spoke of an unspoken transaction, a trade older than the casino itself.

Anna felt a hard knot form in the pit of her stomach. This was the facade of luxury that masked the grim reality of exploitation. And somewhere within this gilded cage, Sahid played puppeteer to these marionettes. She had to find him, had to expose the strings.

If anyone could locate the human trafficker, it was someone involved in the trade.

She moved closer to the trio, her senses alert for any sign of danger, any indication that she had been spotted.

Before she could weave through the crowd to approach them, a human wall materialized before her. The man was an imposing figure; his broad shoulders and jutting chest seemed to stretch his suit to its limits. The seam on his left shoulder had been stressed to the point of snapping. She spotted small threads jutting out like loose hairs on a pubescent upper lip.

"Excuse me," Anna's voice was a calm she did not feel, attempting to sidestep the obstacle.

"Name and room number?" His voice was a deep rumble, echoing the bass of the background music, and his eyes were unyielding, scanning her with professional skepticism.

"I was just—"

"Name and room number," he repeated, his stance unmovable, arms folded across his chest like iron girders reinforcing his presence.

From the corner of her eye, Anna caught sight of the young woman in the red suit with the tablet, her expression transformed from polite hospitality to a creased brow of concern. She stood stiffly behind the counter, hands gripping its edge, her attention darted between Anna and the looming security guard challenging her legitimacy.

Anna's heart pounded in her chest, a stark contrast to the serene expression she painted on her face. The large man's shadow enveloped her as if he were a storm cloud ready to burst.

"Look," she began, her voice smooth, "I'm waiting for someone. He should be here any moment." Her eyes didn't meet his; instead, they flickered past his broad shoulder, feigning the arrival of an imaginary companion.

"Names," he insisted, the word falling like a hammer, demanding compliance.

The casino's ambient light glinted off the golden name tag pinned to his black jacket. Abbot. The giant man stepped towards her, his scowl deepening. "Name and room number, now!" he snapped.

Clearly, the woman behind the counter had sniffed something amiss with Anna, and now, Anna spotted the two prostitutes leading their client away from the table, towards an elevator in the back of the long hall. Both the women were laughing, their bodies draped against the man.

Anna felt a flicker of frustration. Sahid was involved in trafficking. If anyone could give her insight into the underbelly of this place, it would be the two prostitutes. But now... her path was blocked. Her frustration mounted.

"Get out of my way," she said firmly.

But the big man clapped a hand on her shoulder. "You're coming with me," he snapped.

She pretended to stumble, bumping into him. He snapped at her, shoving her back. Without him noticing, though, she yanked the small ballpoint pen cap from his suit pocket. She didn't need the pen. Just the cap.

More specifically, the metal piece attached to the cap. It would serve...

She didn't fight, but instead apologized quickly, and stepped back, her hand concealing her purloined tool.

Chapter 10

The security room in the casino's basement was chilly, and Anna stared at the closed door, waiting until she was sure her captor wasn't returning.

Anna's fingers slipped to her waistband, deftly pulling out the small metal shim she'd taken from the giant's ballpoint pen. She pried it loose from the pen's plastic cap, dropping the cap and gripping the makeshift lockpick. The security door loomed before her. She slid the thin piece of metal into the lock mechanism, applying just the right amount of pressure until she felt the pins give way. A soft *click* heralded her success as the door yielded to her touch.

Inside the security room, shadows clung to every corner. Anna leaned against the cool metal of the door frame, allowing her eyes to adjust to the dim light. She took a moment—a luxury in her line of work—to ensure her exit was calculated.

She peered through the narrow opening she had created. The hallway outside was painted in muted tones of gray and black, washed in the soft glow of overhead lights. She searched for movement, for signs of life, but found none until—

"Dammit, Greeves, if you want it done right, we have to go through everything again," a voice grumbled, echoing off the walls.

Anna froze, her body tensing like a coiled spring. Through the sliver of open space, she caught sight of a towering figure whose size alone commanded attention. The giant security guard, Abbot, who'd brought her here stood with his arms crossed over his broad chest, engaging in conversation with two individuals who could only be Agents Greeves and Jefferson from their crisp suits and stern demeanors.

A thrill of excitement shot through Anna's veins, a silent cheer for the confirmation she sought. If the feds were here, she was on the right track. Unless… they were here for her?

No. No, they wouldn't have been able to take an hour flight in the last ten minutes she'd eben apprehended. They were discussing details she couldn't quite hear, but their very presence here, at this hour, spoke volumes.

But another emotion competed: concern. *Why* were the feds here?

Anna pulled back slightly, pressing herself against the wall. The metal shim, now warmed by her touch, lay hidden once more within her grasp. As she observed the exchange between the guard and the agents, she cataloged every detail—posture, gestures, the subtle shift of their gazes. Every scrap of information was ammunition.

The security room's door hovered at the edge of closing, a barrier between her and the path forward. But Anna had no intention of retreating.

She slipped through the barely ajar door, a ghostly figure against the dimly lit corridor. Her gaze flickered to a vent near the ground, its grate screwed tight but promising an unseen route. Time was her enemy as much as the guards patrolling these restricted halls.

She darted towards it, her steps soundless on the plush carpet, her hands already working to retrieve the shim once more. This time, she turned it sideways, slotting it in the screws. Her fingers worked at the screws, but they resisted her hurried attempts. She cast a furtive glance over her shoulder, acutely aware of how vulnerable she was crouched in the open.

Realizing the vent wouldn't give in time, Anna abandoned her efforts and looked around for another option. A door ajar across the hall beckoned, a sliver of light escaping its confines. Without hesitation, she crossed the threshold, only to freeze as her presence collided with that of three guards stationed within.

She paused, going still.

The room hummed with the low murmur of surveillance equipment. Screens lined the walls, each flickering with parts of the casino's hidden anatomy.

Three men. All security. All facing the monitors.

She pressed her hand against the door, to ease it open, to slip back out.

But then as if sensing her presence, one at a time, they turned. The guards, once relaxed in their routine vigilance, now turned towards Anna like predators alerted to an unexpected prey.

For a moment, the world seemed to pause, suspended in mutual surprise. Their eyes locked with hers.

"Whoopsie, did I take a wrong turn somewhere?" Anna chirped with feigned innocence, her voice rising to a pitch that echoed the frivolity of the Strip outside. She staggered slightly for effect, shoulders slumping and eyes wide, trying to embody every cliché of a tipsy tourist who had stumbled into forbidden territory.

It wasn't common knowledge but the special operatives on her team had spent over a year in professional acting classes: social camouflage was as important as ghillie suits.

The guards exchanged wary glances, their skepticism radiating like heat from asphalt. This was no place for a lost party-goer, and the incongruity of her presence against the backdrop of blinking monitors and coiled wires was glaringly obvious.

"Okay, sweetheart, hang on a moment," the closest guard said as he reached out to grasp her arm.

Anna's muscles tensed beneath her skin, a coiled spring. As his fingers closed around her forearm, she twisted away, pivoting on the ball of her foot. Her other hand shot out, striking the base of his wrist. The sharp snap of tendons preceded his yelp of pain as he recoiled, releasing.

In the space of a heartbeat, the room erupted into chaotic motion. The second guard lunged towards her, a baton raised high. She ducked under its arc, driving her elbow into his gut, forcing the air from his lungs in a single, violent gust and sending him clattering back into the monitors of the security system. His chair toppled, and she kept it between her and the man. He doubled over, gasping, his weapon clattering to the floor.

The third guard, previously hovering by the monitors, stepped over the fallen chair and past his fallen companion, and he advanced with more caution. Three steps. Two. One away. But Anna was already moving, her body remembering the dance of close-quarters combat better than it remembered her own name. She spun, her leg sweeping out in a low arc, catching him behind the knees. He crashed to the ground with a grunt, his arms flailing for balance he couldn't find.

She wasn't a combat sports fighter. She wasn't a *competitor*. She was trained to do exactly one thing.

Two more swift motions, and the threats were neutralized.

Seconds later, the three guards lay sprawled on the carpeted floor, motionless, their breaths shallow and uneven. Anna stood among them, chest heaving softly, her eyes scanning the room for any further threats. Silence settled once again, save for the hum of the computers and her own steady breathing. She allowed not even a whiff of satisfaction. Emotions only muddied the mission. She stepped over the inert forms and pressed onward, her mission far from over.

Anna's gaze snapped to the laminate security card clipped to a downed guard's belt, its edge peeking out. With swift fingers that betrayed no tremor, she liberated it from its holder—a ticket deeper into the lion's den. As she pocketed the card, her mind flashed to the elevator's digital display. The memory from when the security guard had led her away. The small red dot glowing persistently on the twenty-first floor. That was where he had gone—the man flanked by his paid companions, their destination now hers.

Turning away from the incapacitated bodies, Anna's eyes locked onto the bank of monitors, each screen flickering with images of the casino's innards. She knew these cameras were prying eyes she needed to blind. She spotted the half-drunk paper cups of coffee abandoned during the earlier scuffle.

She grasped the cups, their contents still warm, and in a sweeping arc, emptied them over the keyboards and screens. A sizzle of electronics ensued, and the sharp scent of burnt wiring clawed at the back of her throat. She watched for a moment as the screens shorted out, one by one, their surveillance mosaic winking out like stars smothered by dawn.

Now, with the guards down and the eyes of the casino temporarily blinded, she could move freely. It was time to ascend to the twenty-first floor.

Anna's fingers gripped the edge of the vent above the smoking security display, the metal cool against her skin. She hoisted herself up with the lithe grace of a predator climbing through the urban jungle. The vent was cramped, a narrow artery within the casino's concrete heart.

The labyrinth of ducts didn't faze her; she had memorized the blueprints, each twist and turn embedded in her mind like the streets of her childhood neighborhood. The familiar hum of the air conditioning system accompanied her as she crawled, a reminder of the lifeblood of Vegas flowing invisibly around her. Her elbows and knees were relentless pistons, propelling her towards her destination.

Finally, she spied the slatted opening that signaled her exit point. Cautiously lowering herself down, she emerged discreetly near an elevator bank, the soft carpet of the corridor muffling her landing. She rose, adjusting her attire but with no hope of blending in with the outlandish glamour that thrived in the casino.

Anna approached the elevator, slipping the purloined security card from her waistband. She slid it through the reader with the confidence of someone who belonged, the light turning green with an inviting beep. As the doors whispered open, she stepped inside the gilded cage, pressing the button for floor twenty-one.

As the elevator ascended, the flickering digits above the door seemed to synchronize with her racing pulse. Through the metal grate of the elevator door, which allowed viewing of the floors, she watched the floors pass by, catching glimpses of the casino's patrons. A group of raucous bachelors stumbled past, their laughter booming like rolling dice. A woman in a sequined dress leaned heavily on a slot machine, her expression a cocktail of desperation and hope. Each face was a mask, each laugh a bet placed against the house.

The elevator halted with a gentle ding, the sound of arrival. Floor twenty-one loomed before her. As the doors parted, Anna stepped out, her eyes scanning the opulent hallway.

Anna's steps were muted on the plush carpet as she moved from one door to the next, her ears attuned to the slightest hint of the debauchery she was seeking. She paused, leaning subtly against the polished wood of one particular door, where the sounds from within hinted at more than just a game of chance.

Her heart quickened. Anna retrieved the stolen security card, its magnetic strip cool against her fingertips.

Sliding the card into the lock, the LED blinked from red to green, and with a soft click, the door yielded. Anna slipped through the threshold with the confidence of shadow merging with darkness. However, the sight that greeted her made her freeze, her instincts momentarily jarred by the incongruity.

Instead of the tangled web of limbs she anticipated, two older people lay before her, their silver hair moonlit by the dim glow of a bedside lamp. They were lost in an embrace that spoke of years shared, a quiet love far removed from the carnal chaos

Anna had expected to find. For a fleeting second, something akin to guilt pricked at her resolve.

Retreating as silently as she'd entered, Anna closed the door with the gentlest of clicks, her presence in their sanctuary erased like a whisper in a storm. She exhaled slowly, recalibrating, knowing that time was a luxury she couldn't afford.

Anna winced as she stole down the plush corridor, the soft carpet swallowing the sound of her footfalls. The clash of misjudgment lingered in her mind, a reminder that assumptions could be treacherous, even for someone honed by Navy SEAL discipline. Her senses remained on high alert, sifting through the muffled voices and distant laughter that permeated the walls.

"Where are you," she muttered quietly.

A low, rhythmic thumping beckoned her from the end of the hallway, a syncopated heartbeat against the backdrop of Vegas's nocturnal pulse.

The sounds grew more distinct as she approached the penultimate door, the unmistakable cadence of flesh and fantasy behind it, punctuated by soft, feathery swishes and stifled moans. Anna paused, her hand hovering over the security card; this was the moment of truth.

She slid the card home, the lock acquiescing with a soft beep. The door swung inward, revealing the tableau she had been searching for: a man, chained to the headboard of a lavish bed, his eyes wide with a blend of fear and elation. Flanking him were two women clad in little more than shadows and suggestion, feather whips in their hands, orchestrating his ecstasy with every practiced flick.

Anna stepped inside, allowing the door to close behind her with a *click*.

Silence crashed into the room like a wave as Anna's presence registered with the trio. The man on the bed squinted at her, confusion etching his features, while the two women ceased their feathery assault, standing as still as statues in a sketch of sin and satin.

"Who are you?" one of the women demanded, her voice a mix of indignation and surprise, the feather whip hanging limp in her hand.

Anna offered a smile that didn't quite reach her eyes. "Ladies," she said, her tone casual. "We need to chat."

Chapter 11

The man's gaze flickered between Anna and the two women, the chains rattling softly as he shifted. His mouth opened, perhaps to protest or plead, but no words came out, only a breathy gasp that spoke volumes of the night's indulgences.

One of the women stepped forward, defiance rising in her stance. "We don't talk to strangers," she snapped, her eyes narrowing with suspicion.

"Then it's a good thing I'm not here to make friends," Anna replied coolly. She moved closer, each step measured and deliberate, her training honing her senses to any sudden movements. "I just need a moment of your time."

The women exchanged a glance, a silent communication passing between them. It was clear they were weighing their options, deciding whether to scream for help or deal with this unexpected interloper themselves.

"Time is something you might be running out of," Anna added, letting the implication hang heavy in the air.

The two women, scantily clad, were in the midst of dressing now, throwing on their clothing. The garish neon from The Strip spilled through the half-open curtains, casting an unforgiving glow on their hasty movements.

Anna's hand shot out, clutching a crumpled wad of bills. She thrust it toward the women. "A Benjamin," she said, her voice taut with urgency. "Just tell me what you know about Abdo Sahid."

The women both stiffened at the name, as if she'd uttered an expletive. They cast quick glances towards one another.

The nearest prostitute, hair tumbling in a golden cascade over her scantily clad shoulders, let out a derisive snort as she eyed the money. "Honey, we make that tenfold in an hour on a slow night," she said, her lips curling into a sneer. Her companion, still pulling on her thigh-high boots, gave a sharp nod of agreement, her gaze never leaving Anna's.

"Please." Anna's plea sliced through the tension, and she stepped back to press her frame against the door, effectively sealing their only exit. More flies were caught with honey, and these two women weren't the sort of threat she could deal with the usual way. "It's not just about the money. This is important."

The desperation in her voice was raw, unmasked; it was the sound of someone who had too much at stake to walk away empty-handed. Anna watched them, saw the wariness flicker in their eyes. The name Abdo Sahid was a shackle they all wore, whether they liked it or not.

Anna's jaw clenched, the muscle flexing with the effort to keep her composure. Images of Fatima's face, younger and innocent, flashed before her eyes—the same eyes that had looked up at her before the explosion. The ache of loss twisted inside her like a knife, but she pushed it down, deep into the pit of her stomach where all her darkest memories lay. All the people she'd failed… all the souls she'd taken.

"Look," Anna started again, voice steeling as she watched the two women sidle toward the exit, their movements a delicate dance of fear and determination, "I understand you're scared, but if Sahid is here, I need to know where he is."

Her words hung heavy in the air, but the prostitutes seemed unswayed. The golden-haired one reached for the door handle, fingers brushing against the cool metal, but Anna moved faster. In one fluid motion, she slid her wallet from her back pocket and fished out another hundred dollar bill—the last vestiges of her cash reserves.

"Two hundred," she said, extending the crinkled notes toward them. "It's all I have on me, but it's yours if you just give me something—anything."

Even as she said it, standing there... Casper's question resounded in her mind.

Why?

A haunting question. Why. But Anna felt like a shark. She couldn't stop moving, or she'd sink. She'd known this forever. And as much as she loved Beth, and wanted to be near her sister... Anna's home had wheels. She lived in an RV. She'd never married. Never dated anyone seriously, not counting high school flings.

But why?

Her sister was still back home... Her mother still lived alone after what had happened to their father. Anna scowled.

She tried not to think about her family. She'd often told herself that she lived on the road so that others could sleep safe and sound at night, but a part of her wondered if her restless soul was something more than simple altruism.

Sometimes, she feared what might arise if she went still. If she allowed herself to sink to the bottom of the ocean, to where the dark and dingy secrets festered. A flash of images through her mind: a knife in the dark of a Turkish bath. A bullet on the wind towards an unexpecting diplomat. Poison in an East Asian businessman's cup of tea.

How many secrets lay buried deep, deep down?

She shivered. She scorned the question why?

Why not?

Who the hell was going to stop a bastard like Sahid? Not governments. Not agencies. No one.

So *why not* her?

She suppressed the rising tide of thoughts, and instead kept her money extended towards the two women. The man on the bed was still trying to get free, his hands bound above him.

"Well?" she insisted, shifting side to side. Still moving. A shark that refused to sink. That was the damn reason why.

The silence between them stretched, a taut wire ready to snap under the weight of Anna's insistence. Just as the brunette's lips parted, perhaps to spill the secrets Anna so desperately needed, the shrill chirp of Anna's phone sliced through the tension.

Without looking away from the women, she fished the device from her jacket pocket and glanced at the screen.

"Get out NOW. Feds en route to 21st floor," the message from Waldo blazed in stark white against the black background, its urgency undeniable.

Blood roared in Anna's ears, a primal drumbeat urging her to flee. She clenched her jaw, a bitter taste spreading across her tongue.

"Damn it, Waldo," she muttered under her breath, frustration simmering below the surface. How did he know? The possibility that he had disregarded her explicit instructions and infiltrated the hotel despite the risks involved sent a flare of anger through her. They had been clear—no unnecessary moves, no risks that could compromise the mission.

But there was no time to dwell on Waldo's insubordination or the potential fallout it might entail. The ticking clock had just accelerated, and staying meant courting danger, for herself and for the information she still hoped to coax from the prostitutes' reluctant lips.

She refocused on the two women before her, tossing a wad of bills onto the stained motel carpet. Their eyes darted to the money and back up to Anna's steely gaze.

"Talk," Anna demanded. Her voice was low, an undercurrent of urgency betraying the calm she projected.

One of the women hesitated, then crouched to pick up the cash, tucking it securely into the band of her skirt. She glanced at her companion, who remained silent, a tacit agreement passing between them. "We don't know no Abdo Sahid," she confessed in a husky voice, wariness etching her features. "But there's this one guy... Middle Eastern, yeah? Showed up some months back."

Anna leaned in, her attention sharpening. "Go on," she prodded, the weight of every second pressing upon her.

"Two girls went missing," the woman continued, her eyes shifting as if expecting shadows to spring to life. "Dead, they say. And this casino..." She paused, a shudder rippling through her. "It's like he just slid in and took the reins. People are scared, talking under their breaths, ya know?"

The other woman just nodded. "They're saying someone's trying to buy this casino. Lotta money comes through this place, but that's above our pay grade."

Anna tensed. Some casinos pulled as much as ten billion a year. If someone like Sahid had that sort of money... she shivered at the thought of what he might do with it. Who's pocket that money might line back in Yemen.

What could he fund with ten billion dollars? What projects might he involve himself in. She felt a cold shiver along her spine.

"Scared of what?" Anna pressed, her hand inching toward the door in preparation for a swift exit.

A bitter laugh escaped the prostitute's lips. "Calls himself a businessman, but there's nothing legit about him. He's evil, honey. Dangerous in ways that make your skin crawl."

Anna absorbed the words, each one adding weight to the dread pooling in her gut. This man, whether Abdo Sahid or not, was a thread she needed to follow. Abdo Sahid might very easily have used an alias—he wasn't stupid.

Taking a deep breath, Anna steadied her voice. "Where can I find him?" The urgency knotted in her chest, but she held the prostitute's gaze with unwavering intensity.

The woman hesitated, her eyes darting to the half-open window, then back to Anna's face as if measuring the risk of every syllable about to escape her lips. With a nervous twitch, she leaned closer. "Look," she whispered, the word barely audible, "he's got ties, okay? Ties to some sheriff's office. Some tiny speck of a town outside Vegas."

"Where?" Anna urged, her pulse thrumming in her ears.

"Ridge Heel," the prostitute murmured, her alarm clear as she glanced at the door.

Without another word, the women slipped past Anna, their departure swift and silent as shadows fleeing light. Left alone with the information hanging heavy in the air, Anna's thoughts spun. Connections to law enforcement—a sobering revelation that tightened the net around her own investigation.

With no time to waste, Anna eased the door open, peering into the hall.

She hissed under her breath, staring.

Her exit plan was cut short by the sudden sight of dark suits a stark contrast against the hotel's plush carpeting. Panic flared within her, but she tamed it, calculating her next move.

"Hey!" The call came sharply from down the corridor. Special Agent Greeves had spotted her, his hand raised as he moved to intercept. Their eyes locked for an instant—recognition mingled with surprise.

She didn't respond, couldn't afford to.

Greeves' shout was a starting pistol, the stretch of carpet her track. She lunged into a sprint, her heart hammering against her ribs like a frantic drummer in sync with the rapid tattoo of her footsteps. The plush pile muffled her steps as she bolted, but her pulse thundered in her ears.

Voices shouted after her. Jefferson's now. Anna wondered if the hostile agent would try to put a bullet in Anna's back.

The hallway blurred into a streaky tunnel of light and shadow, every door she passed a blur. She could feel the agents now, an electric current of intent at her back, their own urgency fueling her flight.

Her focus narrowed to the green-lit sign of salvation—the stairway. It loomed ahead, a portal to anonymity, to the gritty underbelly of Vegas where she could slip away, become a nameless face in the crowd once more. She skidded around the corner, rubber soles squeaking a brief protest against the polished floor before finding purchase again.

She hit the stairwell door with the force of a fugitive's hope, bursting through it and descending the concrete steps two at a time. The stairwell echoed with the beat of her descent, a rhythm punctuated by the distant shouts that chased her from above.

"Stop!" Greeves' voice lost its edge to the distance, his authority diluted by the echo chamber of stairs and steel.

But Anna wasn't the woman who stopped—not for fear, not for federal badges. Each downward leap took her further from capture, closer to the thin lead on Sahid. Her mind played the information on loop—the small town, the sheriff's office.

She burst out of the emergency exit at the ground level, the alarm shrieking at her passage.

But Anna was already gone, a shadow swallowed by neon.

Chapter 12

The desert night was a black canvas stretched tight over the world, and Anna's grip on the steering wheel matched the rigidity of her jaw.

"Waldo, what were you thinking?" she snapped without taking her eyes off the road. The RV rumbled beneath them, an unwieldy beast barreling toward the small town of Ridge Heel just outside Vegas' opulent reach.

Waldo shifted in his seat, his silhouette slouching against the dim dashboard lights. "Anna, I just needed some air, you know?" His voice had the lilt of a man walking a verbal tightrope, balancing between apology and his innate penchant for taking nothing seriously. "I popped in for a couple of minutes. That's all."

"Air," Anna echoed flatly, her voice edged with sarcasm. "The one thing we have plenty of out here, and you had to leave the RV at the most critical time?"

"If I hadn't, you wouldn't have known about the feds, right?"

Her eyes shifted to the briefcase at his feet. When he'd returned to the RV, two hours ago, she'd heard the clinking sound of what sounded suspiciously like poker chips. She supposed bringing Waldo to Las Vegas was like leading a puppy to a pack of sausages and then leaving it unattended.

She frowned, refocusing.

The desert night lay thick around them as the RV's headlights cut a swath through the darkness, illuminating the road that led to the sheriff's office of the sleepy town. Despite the late hour, the building was ablaze with light, every window a glaring square in the otherwise slumbering facade.

Anna parked the massive vehicle on the opposite side of the road, engine idling softly. The stark contrast between the humble town's usual nocturnal dormancy and the current activity at the sheriff's office wasn't lost on her. Poised in the driver's seat, she took in the scene: multiple sleek black SUVs were lined up out front, their polished surfaces gleaming under the streetlights. They seemed like foreign invaders among the dusty pickups and outdated patrol cars typically found in such a place.

"Looks like we've got company," Waldo murmured, peering through the windshield.

"Yup," Anna replied tersely, her focus fixed on the anomaly before them. Her hand reached for the binoculars wedged between the seats.

Through the magnified lens, she could see figures descending the steps of the sheriff's office—men with stern expressions and purposeful strides, their attire far too formal for a casual visit to a local law enforcement outpost. Their features, caught briefly under the exterior lights, suggested Middle Eastern descent, adding another layer of mystery.

Just off to the side, a group of deputies huddled near one of their service vehicles. Even from this distance, their body language spoke volumes; they shuffled on their feet, arms crossed over chests, faces drawn into scowls. They seemed irritated, disgruntled, but notably refrained from approaching the visitors.

"None of this adds up," Anna said, lowering the binoculars. She felt the chill of the desert night creep into the RV, sensed it not as a drop in temperature but as a foreboding that gnawed at her insides. Something was happening here, something that had no business in a quiet town like this.

Waldo leaned back in his seat, cracking his neck. "You thinking what I'm thinking?"

"Depends on whether you're taking this seriously," she shot back, though her gaze never left the men now re-entering the building.

A ringtone cut through the silence of the RV like a sharp inhale, jarring Anna from her observations. She grabbed the phone, her eyes never leaving the strange scene across the street. "Talk to me, Casper."

"Got something you're not gonna like," came Casper's voice, tense and terse over the line. "Bank records came in. The sheriff's department here? They're swimming in dirty money. Each deputy, a hundred grand. And the big boss? Two mil."

Anna's grip tightened on the phone. "You're sure about this?" she managed, her voice steady.

"Yup."

"How's Beth?"

"Fine. We're training in the morning."

"Good... good. Thanks, Casper."

"She's paying me, Anna. Favor for a friend was spent months ago. This is a job." A pause. "But you're welcome. I'll keep an eye on her."

Anna felt a flicker of relief and ended the call. But now, as she stared towards the office, she felt the weight of corruption suffocating the air around her. This wasn't just small-town politics; it was high-stakes deceit paid for in stacks of hush money.

She let out a breath she hadn't realized she'd been holding and fixed her gaze on the sheriff's office. The deputies' disgruntled postures made sense now—they were bought, all of them. Her mind whirred into action, thoughts ticking like cogs in a well-oiled machine. There had to be a way into that compound, a crack in their armor that she could exploit.

"Everything okay?" Waldo asked, eyeing her. He was leaning back, feet on the dash, hands behind his head. His chair was slightly reclined and he'd somehow managed to procure a cold wine cooler which rest in the cup holder at his side.

He looked the picture of comfort.

"Far from it," Anna replied, her tone sharper than she intended. "But we have to get inside."

"Look," Waldo finally broke the silence, "what if we offer the deputies a better deal? Outbid whoever's lining their pockets?"

Anna shot him a withering glance, the idea slicing through her like a blade. "With what money, Waldo?"

Waldo shrugged, an awkward puppet of a man trying to dance around the problem. "I'm just throwing ideas out."

Anna turned her attention back to the dark road ahead, her thoughts racing faster than the RV's wheels could carry them. She mulled over every possible angle, every resource at her disposal—however meager.

Anna chewed her lip, her gaze distant. The night air slipping through the slightly opened window carried the scent of desert sage and dust.

"Anna, hear me out," Waldo implored, leaning forward in his seat, and his eyes sparkled with an idea that held the same kind of gambler's allure. "I've got skills at the poker table. I can turn a dime into a grand before you can say 'jackpot.'"

Anna's hands tightened around the steering wheel, knuckles whitening. "You're talking about gambling now? That's your grand solution?" Disbelief laced her voice, thick as the dust clouds their wheels kicked up. She shot him a glance that was meant to wilts plants at twenty paces.

"Come on, Anna, it's not like I'm shooting craps with the last of our luck here. I'm good—no, scratch that—I'm phenomenal at cards." Waldo's chest swelled with confidence, and he gave her a lopsided grin that usually disarmed most of his skeptics.

"Phenomenal, huh?" Anna echoed dryly, resisting the urge to roll her eyes. "And when you lose, we end up even deeper in the hole than we are now."

"Ah, but what if I win?" His eyebrows danced.

"Big if," she muttered, but a part of her mind—a desperate, cornered part—wrestled with the possibility. They needed money, and they needed it fast. Could she really afford to dismiss any option, no matter how outlandish?

"Look, Anna, it's this simple: you keep watch while I play. We'll set a limit; I lose more than a grand, and we walk away. But if lady luck kisses my cheek tonight..." He trailed off, leaving the tantalizing thought of success hanging between them.

"Or slaps you for being too fresh," Anna retorted, but the hard line of her mouth softened just a fraction. She hated to admit it, even to herself, but Waldo had a point. Their options were as barren as the desert landscape around them. She couldn't take on a deputy's station without some inside help. And if they were bought off? She needed another way.

"Come on, Anna. What have we got to lose? I'll even front." He tapped the suitcase under his feet.

"I thought you said those were marbles."

"Don't be dumb. We both know these aren't marbles."

She remained motionless, eyes hooded, mind racing. The image of those sleek black SUVs and the corrupt deputies played in her mind, a stark reminder of the stakes they were up against.

"Maybe we gain enough to tilt the playing field back in our favor," Waldo countered, his tone earnest now, stripped of its usual sarcasm.

Anna let out a long breath, feeling the weight of the decision press down upon her shoulders. "Fine," she conceded, the word tasting like defeat and hope all mixed together. "But the moment things go south, we're out of there. Agreed?"

"Agreed," Waldo nodded solemnly, though his eyes danced with the thrill of the challenge.

"Then let's find the nearest place where you can work your so-called magic."

Chapter 13

The lights of the casino flashed in synchronized chaos, attempting to lull its patrons into the belief that time wasn't passing—there were no clocks on the walls, nor windows to view the city beyond. The glow from the warm bulbs above shone, bathing Anna and Waldo's faces in a dance of reds and blues as they stepped through the sliding glass doors from the greeting atrium to the main floor. Waldo, with his square jaw set in determination, clasped the briefcase of poker chips.

Anna trailed behind him, her gaze sweeping over the cavernous room filled with the buzz of slot machines and the faint scent of desperation masked by cologne and perfume. She noted every exit, every face that seemed to linger too long on them, every security camera that panned in their direction. Her hands, hidden in the pockets of her leather jacket, clenched and unclenched rhythmically, mirroring the pounding of her heart.

As they navigated through the forest of blackjack tables and roulette wheels, Anna felt the weight of their plan settle on her shoulders. The briefcase contained not just chips, but the only chance they had at turning a deputy. If they couldn't outbid... Anna would be forced to take more drastic measures.

Waldo moved with the confidence of a man who had done this a hundred times before. He was already making eyes at one of the dealers—a pretty, Asian woman shuffling cards.

She watched him take a seat at the high-stakes poker table, the green felt sea stretching out before them, a battleground where fortunes were won and lost in the blink of an eye.

"Keep it together, Anna," she murmured to herself. Doubt clawed at her insides, images of failure flashing through her mind. What if Waldo's luck ran dry? What if the cards turned against them? They would be left with nothing, their last chance for leverage gone.

With her resolve steeling her nerves, Anna settled into the shadows, her eyes locked onto Waldo.

Waldo was the picture of confidence at the poker table: an easy, leonine smile on his lips, his expression unreadable, eyes hidden behind dark sunglasses that reflected the overhead lights like two distant stars. The chips lay piled in front of him.

As she watched Waldo, though, she noticed something else. Every few minutes, his hand would drift to his ear, a subtle, almost imperceptible movement. To any onlooker, it might seem like a nervous tick or an absent-minded scratch.

She caught him glancing upwards repeatedly, too, his eyes flicking to the ornate ceiling with its intricate patterns of gold leaf and crystal chandeliers. Was he searching for something? Or someone? A wave of suspicion washed over her, and she tucked a strand of hair behind her ear, pretending to adjust her position while keeping a covert watch on Waldo.

As the poker game commenced, Anna scanned the table, her keen eye taking in the assortment of players gathered around Waldo. On his immediate right sat a man with a hawkish nose, his fingers adorned with rings that glittered under the casino lights. His playing style was aggressive, each bet thrown down with a clatter.

Next to him was a woman with sharp cheekbones, her raven-black hair cascading down her back. She played her cards close to her chest, her expression unreadable—impassive as a statue. Her bets were measured, calculated moves in a game of chess rather than chance.

Across from Waldo, a hulking figure with forearms like steel cables studied his hand with intense concentration. He had the patience of a predator, waiting for the perfect moment to strike. When he did place a bet, it was with a deliberate force that made the chips clink menacingly against one another.

And then there was Waldo, the enigma at the center of it all. He held his cards with casual ease, a faint smile playing on his lips as if he were merely enjoying a friendly game at a backyard barbecue. Yet, beneath that veneer of nonchalance, Anna sensed a coiled readiness, an alertness that belied his relaxed posture. His hand would still occasionally rise towards his ear, and each time, Anna's frown deepened.

The cast of characters at the table wove a tapestry of bluff and double-bluff, of daring and caution.

Above the soft hum of conversation, the rhythmic shuffle of cards formed a persistent undertone, a heartbeat driving the pulse of the casino. Anna's gaze swept across the sea of green felt tables, each a small arena where fortunes were contested. A cocktail waitress moved through the throng, her tray laden with liquid courage that fueled the bravado at the tables.

Anna watched as a dealer deftly fanned out a new deck, bridging the cards in a fluid motion that seemed like sleight of hand. Nearby, a player tapped his stack of chips against the table—once, twice—a beat that heralded a bold raise.

She winced as Waldo shoved in the majority of his chips. Five grand. All he had.

She shifted from foot to foot as Waldo revealed one, then two Kings.

The man with the steel-cable arms hesitated, then cursed, flinging down his cards to reveal he'd flopped a second queen.

"Damn luck," the man muttered under his breath, glaring at Waldo.

Suddenly, the low murmur of the crowd shifted, subtly changing tempo. Security guards, indistinct in their uniform black suits, began their silent patrol among the glittering slot machines and card tables. Anna's heart hitched, her eyes tracking their movements with covert intensity. Every muscle in her body tensed, ready to spring into action should they show any sign of interfering with Waldo's game.

But the guards continued on, their eyes scanning the room with practiced detachment. They seemed to be looking for trouble but finding the evening's play surprisingly orderly. Their presence was a reminder of the casino's unspoken rule: so long as the house's interests were undisturbed, the games would go on.

As they passed by without a second glance at Waldo's table, Anna allowed herself a momentary exhale—a whisper-thin release of breath she hadn't realized she'd been holding. Her focus returned to the table, to Waldo and the dance of deception playing out before her.

Waldo's eyes, sharp as the edge of a dealt card, never wavered from the game. Anna watched him with a mix of admiration and suspicion, leaning against the cool wall in the casino's dimly lit corner.

He sat confidently, his back straight, fingers casually riffing chips. The pile of chips at his hand was growing. Waldo was on a winning streak.

"Keep it casual, just another night," Waldo had said earlier, but there was nothing casual about the way he raked in pot after pot. The other players were no amateurs; their faces were stoic masks, schooled to betray nothing. Yet, one by one, they succumbed to whatever invisible force Waldo wielded.

Anna couldn't shake off the sense of dread that crept up her spine. How did he do it? Was it sheer luck, or something more calculated? She knew Waldo was good – but this good? His calm demeanor and steady hands painted the picture of a seasoned player, but Anna's instincts screamed that there was more at play than skill alone.

Then, it happened.

The air seemed to thicken as Waldo peered at his cards, then at the amassed chips in the center of the table. It was a significant pot, one that could solidify his lead even further. Players leaned in, tension etching deeper lines into their focused expressions. The clinks of chips faded into a background murmur, anticipation charging the atmosphere like static before a storm.

Without warning, Waldo exhaled softly and pushed his cards forward, face-down. "Fold," he stated, his voice unruffled, reasonable almost, as if discussing the weather rather than abandoning a mountain of chips.

A collective gasp rippled through the surrounding observers, their expressions a blend of shock and confusion. Anna's heart stuttered in her chest. To fold now? After such dominance? She scrutinized Waldo's face for any sign of distress, any hint of the turmoil that must surely be churning beneath that composed exterior. There was none. Only the placid, unreadable mask that gave nothing away.

With the fold complete, the tension broke like a snapped string, conversation and the clatter of chips swelling once more to fill the void left by the unresolved mystery of Waldo's play.

Anna's gaze sharpened as she observed Waldo, the subtle yet deliberate gestures he made – a hand brushing an earlobe, a quick tap at his temple. She frowned, her suspicion unfurling like a dark cloud over her thoughts. Each motion seemed too rehearsed, too intentional to be dismissed as mere nervous tics. There was a pattern to it, a coded language of touch that Waldo seemed to be speaking silently.

"Who are you talking to?" she muttered under her breath, her eyes tracing the path of his fingers as they ghosted once more to his ear.

Anna edged away from the electric hum of the poker table, slipping between clusters of onlookers and the occasional cocktail waitress. Her movements were casual, a gambler merely seeking a quieter corner or perhaps a fresh drink, but her intent was laser-focused.

Once safely out of earshot and tucked into the shadowy embrace of a nearby alcove, she retrieved her burner phone. Her thumb hovered over the keypad before pressing the familiar sequence of numbers for Casper. The call connected, and she didn't bother with pleasantries.

"Are you on comms with Waldo?"

There was a pause – too long, too telling – and then Casper's voice, smooth as always, yet tinged with something that didn't sit right with Anna.

"Is everything okay, Anna? You sound tense."

"Cut the crap, Cas. Are you feeding him info?"

"Information is the currency of success," Casper replied, the non-answer hanging between them.

"Damn it, Casper." She glanced around, her eyes catching the slow orbit of a security camera overhead. Its lens swept across the casino floor in a lazy, circling motion, but its watchful gaze felt anything but casual. It might as well have been an all-seeing eye, and she knew that Casper, with his knack for surveillance work, would be watching.

"Be careful," she warned, a thread of frustration coloring her tone. "They're watching. We're not the only ones playing games here."

"Understood," Casper said, and the line went dead, leaving Anna staring at the phone, the weight of the situation pressing down on her. She slipped the device back into her bag and turned her attention back to the game, to Waldo, and the ever-present cameras that saw too much.

In Vegas, cheaters suffered. Especially if someone cheated at cards.

Waldo wasn't just risking cash… he was risking the odds of making enemies. And enemies were the sort of thing one couldn't afford in Vegas.

Anna's gaze flickered back to the poker tables, watching as Waldo raked in another massive pot. The camera continued its relentless sweep above—Casper's eyes in the sky.

"Unbelievable," she muttered under her breath, clenching her jaw as Waldo flashed his trademark grin at the dealer. With each win, he seemed to grow bolder, stacking chips with the casual arrogance of someone who had forgotten how much was on the line.

She could feel the tension thickening in the air, as palpable as the scent of spilled whiskey and desperation that lingered in the dim corners of the casino. Anna kept her arms crossed, a defensive posture that countered the anxiety clawing at her insides. She knew they were deep into dangerous waters; Waldo's streak of luck was a beacon, drawing unwanted scrutiny.

"Keep it together, Waldo," she breathed, though she knew he couldn't hear her silent plea.

As if on cue, a pair of security guards paused nearby, their eyes sharp and assessing. One tapped his earpiece, nodding as though receiving some silent instruction, before they continued their patrol.

She inched closer to the table, trying to appear nonchalant. Waldo's fingers danced across his chips with the finesse of a seasoned magician.

Every chip he stacked higher made her pulse race faster. "Too much attention, Waldo," she thought fiercely. They needed the money, yes, but not at the cost of getting caught.

But Waldo was in his element, surrounded by the felt and the flicker of cards. Every move was a statement, every bet a declaration that he was untouchable. And Anna knew then, with a sinking feeling, that pulling him away from the table would be like coaxing a gambler away from his addiction—with great difficulty and even greater risk.

Anna's resolve crystallized as she watched another hand play out. The stakes were rising, and with it, so did the risk of lingering under the casino's watchful eyes. She leaned into Waldo, her breath a hushed urgency against his earlobe. "We need to leave. Now."

Security was watching them closely now. Three men, staring directly at Waldo.

Shit.

She'd spotted the two backup guards too late. Behind them, coming through the row between slot machines.

"We need to go," she said more firmly.

Waldo's jaw set stubbornly as he shuffled his chips, the sound crisp in the tense silence. "One more hand," he murmured back, the words almost lost amidst the symphony of the casino's nightlife.

She felt the coiled tension in his body, a spring wound too tight. Her fingers found his wrist and clamped down, nails pressing into skin—a silent counterargument meant to convey the danger they couldn't afford to ignore.

The guards were beginning to move now, frowning suspiciously.

For a moment, he seemed to consider her unspoken warning. Then, with a sigh that held the weight of regret, he stacked his final chips and pushed them away from him, folding the hand he had wanted to play. They both stood, and Waldo began to collect their winnings, his movements suddenly brisk, efficient.

The security guards sidled closer, their eyes sharp beneath the brims of their hats. They tracked every motion of Waldo and Anna. The pair could feel the surveillance like a physical touch, cold and calculating.

"Let's go," Anna whispered again, urgency lacing her tone.

Waldo gathered his chips into the same briefcase he'd brought them in. "It's been fun, pals," he said airily. "Thanks for the ride."

"Going so soon?" said the angry man with the thick forearms.

"You know how it is... nagging wench needs me," he said with a nudge at Anna. She resisted the urge to crack his elbow.

Waldo muttered under his breath as Anna finally managed to extricate him and lead him away. "Why you gotta ruin the fun?"

"Your fun is attracting too much attention," she retorted. "Don't look at them."

The security guards didn't stop them, but just watched, frowning.

Together, they navigated through the forest of slot machines and gaming tables, a stream cutting through bedrock, towards the cashier. Waldo placed the mountain of chips on the counter, and the cashier eyed them, her hands a blur as she counted and recounted. When she finally pushed the stacks of bills across the marble surface, they totaled nearly three hundred thousand dollars.

"Congratulations," the cashier said with a professional smile that didn't reach her eyes.

"Today's our lucky day," Waldo replied, his voice like a child's in a candy store.

With the bundle of cash now discreetly enclosed in Waldo's briefcase, they walked away from the cashier's window, each step measured and even. The security guards' gaze followed them until the very threshold of the casino, where the bright lights of the gaming floor gave way to the relative darkness of the night outside.

Anna only released a pent up breath when she decided the guards weren't following her.

Stepping into the tepid night air, Waldo's eyes sparkled like the neon lights that blinked overhead. He clutched the unremarkable suitcase, a poor disguise for the fortune it contained. "Anna, can you believe this? We could just... disappear."

Anna's gaze remained fixed ahead, her jaw set in determination. "Not an option," she said curtly. Pulling him to an alcove shadowed from the prying eyes of the casino, she reached into her jacket pocket.

"Hey, what are you—" Waldo began, but his question was cut short as Anna snapped the cold steel cuffs around his wrist with a decisive click, then fastened the other end around her own.

"What the hell!" he tried to pull his wrist away. The cuff went taut. He glared at her. "No! I don't want to go to prom with you! No means no!"

"Shut up, Waldo."

"Really?"

"Last time I left you unattended, you snuck into a casino," she retorted. "This way, I'll keep an eye on you."

He muttered darkly under his breath.

Waldo's shoulders slumped in resignation, the thrill of the win dimming in his eyes. "Fine, but are these really necessary?" He jangled the chain for emphasis.

"Absolutely," Anna replied, the weight of their mission pressing down on her. "We do this my way."

He sighed, giving the cuff a tug, testing its hold. It didn't budge. A half-smile tugged at the corner of his mouth – part admiring, part exasperated. "You always were the cautious one."

"Someone has to be," Anna countered, her eyes scanning the darkness beyond the casino's glow. She stepped forward, and Waldo followed, the metal links chiming softly between them. Together, they made their way to the RV parked in the shadows, ready to face the long drive back to the small town where a deputy awaited.

They had no other options. The bribe would simply have to work.

Chapter 14

Anna's foot pressed hard against the accelerator, the engine of the old RV roaring in response as it tore along the deserted country road. The moon hung like a silver medallion in the night sky, barely illuminating the dense woods flanking either side of the winding asphalt. Despite the darkness, Anna's eyes remained fixed ahead, unyielding as the handcuff that bit into her flesh, securing the briefcase to her wrist.

She'd agreed to uncuff Waldo but had switched his cuff to the source of his greatest desire: the case full of cash.

The leather of the steering wheel creaked under Anna's white-knuckled grip, the briefcase a metal anchor reminding her of the weight of the task at hand. Every jolt of the car over the uneven road sent a shiver through the chain, a cold, metallic whisper against the silence that filled the vehicle.

"We've been at this for hours," Waldo moaned where he was sulking in the passenger seat.

Anna shot him a sidelong glance. "We've been driving for like twenty minutes, Wally."

He bristled at the nickname. "Back and forth, back and forth," he muttered. "What's the point?"

"Hang tight," she said. But only after she jerked her steering wheel sharply and Waldo's head thumped against the window.

"Hey!"

She smirked.

She floored the pedal again, the decommissioned tank's engine roaring as it carried her RV across the dusty road outside Ridge Heel.

The small town was quiet in the night. Dark. The windows blacked out, and the buildings silent, unlike the neon city they'd left behind.

Suddenly, in the rearview mirror, red and blue lights sliced through the night, painting the interior of the car with an ominous glow. "There we go," she muttered under her breath, glancing at the speedometer which now felt like an accusation.

"Are you kidding me?" Waldo's voice cracked from the passenger seat, his body stiffening, the muscles in his jaw clenching visibly in the sporadic light. "Cops. It's always cops."

"This was the point," Anna said, shooting him a look. "You didn't realize that?"

"Oh... umm... yeah. No... sure."

This was what they'd wanted. Baiting a deputy.

"Relax," Anna murmured, a quiet command that sliced through Waldo's spiraling fear as she eased off the accelerator and steered the car onto the gravel shoulder. Dust billowed behind them, ghostly in the cherry-red glow of the brake lights. She killed the engine, inhaling for three seconds, exhaling for five, keeping herself calm.

Waldo's breaths came in shallow bursts beside her, but Anna kept her gaze fixed on the rearview mirror, watching as the deputy emerged from his vehicle. He was a man caught between youth and middle age, his uniform hanging slightly loose on his frame, as if he had yet to grow into the authority it commanded. The night air, thick with the scent of pine and damp earth, seemed to weigh heavily upon his shoulders, bending his posture into a slight hunch as he approached.

In the beam of his flashlight, his face was a landscape of doubt, eyes darting from the car's license plate to the occupants shrouded within. The lines around his mouth were etched with the fatigue of uncountable hours spent patrolling the sleepy byways of Ridge Heel, where the unexpected was an unwelcome guest. His hand rested near his holster—not quite touching, but close enough to suggest a readiness instilled by protocol rather than intent.

"Evening," he called out, his voice betraying a tremor that the cold night alone could not justify. The beam of light danced nervously across Anna's face, then dropped quickly, as if the deputy feared the illumination might reveal too much. His Adam's apple bobbed in a swallow meant to steady nerves made jittery by the desolation of this nocturnal encounter.

Anna's response was a nod, calm and measured.

The flashlight's quivering ray fell upon the metallic whisper of handcuffs, their glint stark against the leather of the briefcase and the pale of Anna's wrist. The sight snagged the deputy's attention like a barb, his eyes narrowing beneath the brim of his hat.

"Ma'am, what's with the briefcase?"

"Would you believe me if I said it was just paperwork?" She inhaled again. Held the breath. Exhaled.

Calm. In control. She didn't allow nerves to intrude.

The deputy's hand twitched, betraying a flicker of instinct as his fingers grazed the butt of his service revolver. His posture stiffened.

"Hardly seems like paperwork requires handcuffs," he managed to say, though the tremble from earlier hadn't quite left him.

"Sometimes, it's not about what's inside the briefcase," Anna said, locking eyes with the unsettled man before her, "but rather, what it represents. Tell me, Deputy, how much do you have in your bank account right now?"

The question hung in the air, audacious and intrusive, like the piercing hoot of an owl in the stillness of the forest. His Adam's apple jumped again, a visible cue of his discomfort as his fingers settled more decidedly on the grip of his gun, the leather of the holster creaking under the strain.

"You don't have to answer that," she said softly. "But let's talk hypotheticals for a second. Imagine a sum of money that could change your life, no more long nights on these empty roads."

The man's eyes, previously narrowed with duty, now widened with a mix of curiosity and calculation. The night's chill seemed to seep into the car, wrapping its cold fingers around them both as an unspoken proposition dangled precariously in the air.

"An internal investigation is a nasty business," Anna continued, her voice steady despite the adrenaline that coursed through her veins. "Rumors, paperwork, your career on the line... Or you could make a choice tonight that would ensure none of that ever touches you."

The deputy's stance shifted imperceptibly, his weight moving from one foot to the other in the gravel by the roadside.

"I don't know what the hell you're talking about."

"Nah. See. An innocent man would've arrested me by now. You... you know what I'm talking about. A hundred grand. Dropped in your account. Same as the others, right? I'm sure you didn't want to, but how could you say no?"

He stared at her, gaping. "Who are you?" his hand was now tense on his trigger.

She smirked, glancing down and up again, a wolfish smile on her face. She liked this part, when the predator realized he was the prey. Her mind flickered to Fatima. To Abdo Sahid.

Her smile vanished. "A gift," she said simply. "Double up. Why put yourself in harm's way, huh?"

"More cash?" His words were barely audible, a whisper torn away by the wind that rustled the nearby trees. He glanced back toward his patrol car, isolated in the pool of light from its headlights, then back to Anna, seeking something in her face.

Anna felt her pulse in the cuff encircling her wrist, the briefcase an anchor in this high-stakes gamble. Her other hand, concealed from the deputy's view by the dark fabric of the door, rested on the cool metal of her gun.

"Think about it," she urged, her thumb tracing the trigger guard where it rested out of sight. "It's not just about avoiding the bad; it's about embracing an opportunity. One that doesn't come around often."

The deputy's jaw clenched, and his eyes darted away, scanning the darkness as though searching for an answer in the quiet wilderness. For a long moment, there was only the sound of the wind and the distant call of a nocturnal bird. When he finally looked back at Anna, his expression was unreadable, but the indecision had melted into something else – something that resembled resolve.

"Watch," Waldo's voice was a whisper, a rustle of leaves against the hush of darkness. With a deft click, he released the clasp of the briefcase. Its jaws parted slowly, like the opening scene of a play where the curtains draw back.

Beneath the dome light of the car, the cash gleamed. Neat stacks of bills, bundled with precision, filled the case to the brim. The scent of fresh paper lingered in the air, mingling with the musky odor of the leather interior. It was more money than the deputy had ever seen outside of a bank vault, more than he could earn in years of honest work. Anna watched him drink in the sight, her finger still curled on the trigger, like a cobra coiled and waiting to strike.

The deputy swallowed audibly, his Adam's apple bobbing as desire warred with duty. His hand, which had hovered near the butt of his gun, trembled faintly before falling slack at his side. Moonlight spilled across his face.

"She's insane, you know," Waldo murmured. "She really is. Trust me. You took cash once before. Save yourself and your family the trouble. Last time I saw her?" he said, nodding at Anna. "Was in the burnt-out husk of a single family home. Two bodies on the ground." He nodded knowingly.

The deputy swallowed. "Wh-what..."

"Her own family," Waldo said, wagging his head up and down and crossing a finger over his heart solemnly. Anna shot him a sharp glance, frowning. While Waldo was telling the truth, technically, his implications were all lies.

She hadn't caused the fire, she'd discovered it. And the bodies had belonged to two thugs who'd been involved in the arson.

But Waldo's words seemed to be working. One benefit of working with a con-man was he seemed to know what levers to pull to entice the sin of avarice.

The deputy frowned, hesitated...

Then, the subtlest of movements—a taut nod, barely perceptible, yet monumental in its implication.

Anna exhaled slowly, the tension unwinding from her shoulders. "What do you need me to do?" The deputy's voice was rough, like gravel kicked up by passing tires.

"First," Anna began, the corner of her mouth ticking up in a half-smile that didn't reach her wary eyes, "we need trust. Turn off your radio," Anna instructed, her voice steady but edged with the remnants of adrenaline. She watched his face for signs of hesitation, but there were none. He stepped back, and through his window reached for the console and complied, the static hiss of the radio dying abruptly.

"Give me the cash."

"It's yours. But first things first. Listen closely." She called out the window, her eyes scanning the shadows that hugged the edges of the cruiser's headlights. "And do everything exactly how I tell you."

Chapter 15

Sweat beaded on Anna's forehead, the space around her constricted like a vise. The darkness of the deputy's trunk was absolute, a small universe where only the sound of her careful, controlled breaths seemed to exist—until the voices from outside pierced her solitary cocoon. She lay motionless, a statue save for the white-knuckled clutch on the gun, its cold metal a grim comfort.

Outside, the muffled sounds became coherent. Words woven with authority and demand sliced through the air. Anna's jaw clenched, her ears straining to dissect the conversation, to predict what would come next. Could she trust the deputy, driving the trojan horse? The interior of the trunk smelled of old fast food, and she had shoved a couple of fries away from her face after first acclimating to the dark, cramped space.

But she'd been in worse situations before, and now she listened intently.

"Everything okay here, Deputy?" The inquiry was sharp, edged with suspicion.

"Y-yes, just routine," stammered the deputy, his voice quivering slightly—a crack in his facade that did not go unnoticed by Anna. She visualized his face, the way his eyes darted too quickly, how his Adam's apple bobbed with tension.

The deputy had seemed sincere when he'd accepted the bribe, but fear was a powerful adversary.

Through the narrow slit of visibility between the trunk's lid and frame, Anna caught sight of the men in dark suits. They stood like sentinels, their silhouettes rigid against the amber glow of a nearby streetlamp. The faintest glint of light danced off something metallic in the hand of one—a watch, perhaps, or something far more sinister.

The night air carried their cologne, a mix of musk and menace that crept through the car's seams and into Anna's cramped haven. She imagined them as predators, circling, their eyes coldly calculating. Her finger caressed the cool metal of the gun.

A low rumble underlined the sound of a heavy gate rolling on its tracks. The voices that had been so near, so immediate, now carried from beyond that gate, growing fainter with each passing second. The murmurs interlaced with the creaks and groans of the opening barrier.

They were moving through the gate... She released a slow pent up breath she hadn't realized she'd been holding.

Anna strained to listen, to understand the tide of words ebbing away, but they were whispers lost in the wind. The gate's final clang echoed.

A coil of unease unwound within her, tensing the muscles along her spine.

Anna shifted minutely, her body preparing without thought for what might come next.

Then...

Sound.

The world outside the trunk erupted into chaos, a symphony of raised voices clashing like cymbals in the confined space.

A hand pounded on the trunk.

Each thump on the trunk was a thunderclap, resonating through the hollow of the car and into her bones. Anna's fingers tightened around the gun, the weapon's hard edges biting into her palm—a stark reminder of the reality she might be forced to confront.

"Get out with your hands up!" A voice cut through the tumult, authoritative and cold. It wasn't the deputy's voice. This realization was a splash of ice water, jolting Anna from her tense stillness.

"I said get out. Now!" the voice yelled, and she heard the sound of a gun being cocked.

Anna set her teeth, tense and preparing for what came next.

Chapter 16

The car's engine hummed a steady rhythm as it rolled towards the checkpoint. Furkan's gaze, sharp and probing, fixed on the approaching vehicle. The light from the moon glinted off the windshield, but not enough to obscure his view of the man behind the wheel. He recognized Deputy Larkin immediately.

Furkan had come along with some of Sahid's other men. They'd been stationed at this God-forsaken town. Lured to the cursed place by promises of Vegas and its splendor, but then tricked into this backwater dump.

He was already in a bad mood.

Furkan leaned against the barricade, arms crossed, eyes narrowed into slits. As the car inched closer, he could see the deputy's profile, the way his Adam's apple bobbed with an uneasy swallow. Sweat glazed Larkin's forehead, despite the mildness of the night. His knuckles were white on the steering wheel, his glance darting and jittery like that of a cornered animal.

"Stop the car," Furkan said, his voice low and authoritative, cutting through the hum of the idling engine and distant chatter.

Larkin complied, rolling to a stop with a crunch of gravel beneath tires. The deputy fumbled with the window button, a tremor in his fingers as the glass descended with a mechanical whirr.

"Deputy," Furkan started, his tone edged with faux cordiality, "you seem... agitated. Everything alright?"

"Y-Yes, everything's fine, Furkan," Larkin stammered, attempting a smile that faltered before it fully formed. "Just the heat, you know? It's making me sweat more than usual."

"Is that so?" Furkan's voice was ice over steel, his disbelief palpable. He peered into Larkin's eyes, searching for the telltale flicker of deceit. "Because you look like a man who's seen a ghost, deputy."

Furkan glanced back to his other men. All of them stood in their dark suits, watching, waiting. Furkan was their chosen spokesperson, as his English was flawless. But he knew it made the others resent him. Still, he forced a smile back at his companions, and returned his attention to the deputy.

Larkin licked his lips, offering a nervous chuckle that didn't reach his eyes. "Just routine patrol. You know how it is."

"Routine," Furkan repeated the word as if tasting something sour. He released a slow breath, letting the silence stretch between them, heavy with unspoken accusations. Larkin shifted in his seat, his anxiety a scent in the air, tangible and thick.

"Of course," Furkan finally said, stepping back but not breaking eye contact. "I'm sure it's nothing... But you know what happens to those who aren't honest with me, right, deputy?"

A nod, almost imperceptible, betrayed Larkin's understanding. Furkan's suspicion grew roots, tangling and dark. There was a lie here, wrapped in the guise of routine, and he intended to uncover it.

The blade glinted in the sun, a silent threat as Furkan drew it from his belt. His fingers wrapped tightly around the handle, a casual menace that came to him as easily as breathing. He leaned forward, the tip of the knife playing a dangerous rhythm against the metal windowsill, a sharp counterpoint to Larkin's ragged breaths.

"Maybe you need a little reminder," Furkan murmured, his eyes never leaving Larkin's face. "A nudge towards the truth."

Larkin's gaze flickered from the blade to Furkan's unyielding stare, and then, with a subtle twitch of his jaw, he nodded jerkily towards the back of the vehicle, his Adam's apple bobbing with swallowed fear.

Furkan paused, the tap-tap of the knife ceasing as he processed the deputy's silent admission. His mind raced, recalling a chilling memory—a scene stained with blood and punctuated by screams. The merchandise—a term so cold for something alive—had slipped through their grasp earlier today. And the guard, poor, foolish Dalton, had paid the price. They'd recovered the merchandise, however... Jacinth? Was that her name. Now at the race track. He'd handled the issue...but if something else happened?

Something else on his watch?

He shivered. Sahid wouldn't be happy.

Furkan wrinkled his nose, staring at the trunk. He glanced at the deputy, flashed a crocodile smile and held a finger to his lips.

Furkan's shadow loomed large as he advanced on the back of the car, his silhouette etched sharply against the stark glow of the checkpoint's floodlights. A crisp gesture from his hand cut through the tension-thick air, summoning two stone-faced men from the fold of his waiting entourage. They fell into step behind him, their postures rigid with anticipation, fingers instinctively resting near concealed holsters beneath their jackets.

The deputy's eyes, wide and darting, flickered in the rearview mirror, watching the approach, his pallor deepening to a sickly shade. Furkan noted the tremble in the man's hands as they clung to the steering wheel.

"Open it," Furkan ordered, his voice low, the command more a growl than a phrase. He stood back, allowing one of his men, a hulking figure named Idris, to take the lead. The guard rapped a solid knuckle against the trunk lid, the metallic thunks echoing ominously in the night.

"Hands where I can see them!" Idris bellowed at the unresponsive metal barrier. "Come out with your hands up!"

But there was nothing. No shuffling from within, no resigned sigh of compliance—only the oppressive silence that seemed to mock their demands. A bead of sweat traced a path down Furkan's temple, defying the night's chill. His fingers tingled with the memory of cold steel, the weight of the knife now absent but its impression still seared into his palm.

He missed the nights he spent back at the race track. Spending time with the girls when Sahid wasn't looking. They were so... soft and compliant.

He smiled at the memories. But now he was *here*. He scowled at the trunk, as if the vehicle itself was responsible for this strange twist of fate.

The seconds dragged on like hours, each tick of the clock a muffled drumbeat to his racing heart. The stillness held a breath, and for a moment, Furkan felt as though time itself had paused—suspended on the precipice of revelation.

Then, he raised his gun, pointed at the trunk and began to fire.

As the shots rang out in the night, a chorus of echoes bouncing off the surrounding buildings, the air crackled with tension. The metallic thuds of bullets striking metal filled the space. Furkan's jaw clenched, his gaze unyielding as he emptied the clip into the trunk.

The smell of gunpowder lingered, mingling with the heavy scent of dread that hung between them. Larkin flinched at each shot, his eyes wide with a mix of horror and realization.

After the last bullet had been fired and silence descended once more, Furkan stepped forward. With a sharp gesture, he signaled for Idris to open the trunk. The hulking figure obeyed, muscles tensing as he gripped the edge and lifted it open slowly.

"Pop the trunk," Furkan's voice was a blade, sharp and commanding, slicing through the thick tension.

The deputy, his face now a canvas of fear, fumbled with the keys before finally triggering the release. The trunk lid sprang open with an abrupt creak that seemed far too loud in the charged silence. Furkan stepped forward, his men flanking him, all eyes fixed on the gaping maw of the trunk space.

It was empty.

Nothing but the dark velvet lining, marred by the jagged tear where the divider to the back seat had been kicked out. No contraband, no smuggled goods, no person lying in wait—just an ominous void and that ripped fabric like a wound.

"Impossible..." Furkan murmured, his instincts screaming at him. He peered into the shadows of the car's interior.

And then he saw it.

Through the ragged gap where the divider once stood, the lethal black sheen of a gun barrel glinted, pointed directly at him. His breath caught in his chest.

Furkan's survival instincts flared to life, every nerve in his body coiling tight as a spring. The realization hit him like a physical blow. The stowaway had kicked out the divider and snuck into the back seat.

Without warning, the stillness shattered. Gunshots punctured the air, rapid and precise, the sound ricocheting off the concrete walls of the checkpoint. Two of Furkan's men—veterans hardened by countless encounters—crumpled to the ground before anyone could register what had happened. The figure in the back seat was a blur of movement.

Furkan's pulse hammered in his ears, his own training kicking in as he ducked instinctively, taking cover behind the vehicle. His mind raced to make sense of the chaos, but his thoughts were cut short by another swift act of violence. The deputy, still seated in the driver's seat, jerked violently, a thin red line appearing across his throat as if drawn by an invisible artist. Blood blossomed on his uniform, dark and spreading, as he slumped against the wheel lifelessly.

The woman—the assassin concealed within the car's shadows—moved with lethal intent. She didn't hesitate, didn't pause to survey her handiwork. Instead, she leaned over the deputy's body, her hands already finding the gear shift amidst the crimson. The engine roared to life, growling as she threw the vehicle into motion.

Three of Furkan's men had been stationed on the stairs, weapons ready, their eyes locked on the unfolding horror. They braced themselves, ready to intercept, but they were mere obstacles in her path. The car lunged forward, slamming into the trio with bone-jarring force. Bodies were flung aside, cries of pain lost in the screeching of tires against pavement.

Furkan rose from his crouch, disbelief etched on his features as he witnessed the carnage.

And as the dust settled, the realization sank into Furkan's bones: they were not hunting her—she was hunting them.

Furkan's finger tensed on the trigger, his aim locked onto the car as it careened toward the station. His men, dazed and struggling to rise, were scattered obstacles in the car's wake.

He squeezed the trigger. Bullets punctured the evening air, metallic bites seeking flesh. But his target was not where he had aimed; she was a specter of movement, a blur of lethal grace. The car skidded, avoiding the first salvo. Then stopped. A second later, the woman unfolded from the shattered window, contorting her body with the fluidity of smoke escaping a bottle. She emerged onto the car's roof.

Two more of Furkan's men advanced, their weapons upraised, their faces masks of determination. They didn't stand a chance. She moved amongst them like a tempest, her hands instruments of precise violence. A swift kick sent one sprawling, his gun skittering across the concrete. An elbow found the second man's throat, collapsing his windpipe with an efficiency that was almost surgical.

The shouts that erupted from within the police station clawed at Furkan's attention. He swung around, his senses sharpening, trying to pierce the walls that now concealed the pandemonium inside. The solid structure of law and order had become a veil behind which chaos reigned. His mind raced—how many men did he have stationed within?

The woman was already moving, her silhouette a vanishing wisp as she disappeared into the yawning mouth of the station's entrance. Furkan felt a cold dread settle in his stomach, replacing the inferno of battle rage. With every shout that echoed off the walls, with every muffled shot that followed, the danger multiplied, became more real.

Furkan's fingers fumbled for his phone, the device suddenly a slippery eel in his shaking hands. Sweat beaded on his brow, mingling with the dust and grime of the skirmish that had erupted only moments before.

"Damn it," he hissed under his breath, swiping at the screen with an urgency born of fear—a sentiment he hadn't tasted in years, not since he'd clawed his way to his current standing. The numbers blurred before his eyes, a jumbled code that mocked his panic. Finally, his thumb pressed down, holding Sahid's contact as if it were a lifeline.

"Pick up, pick up," he muttered, a mantra against the chaos. He willed his boss to answer, to bring reinforcements, to restore order to the sudden anarchy that had claimed his dominion.

The ringtone droned on, each tone slicing through the madness of the scene around him—a soundtrack to his desperation. Then, a click, and the line opened.

Chapter 17

Anna's boots padded softly against the gritty tile floor of the dimly lit corridor as she stalked through the police station, leaving corpses on the stairs behind her.

The sliding doors couldn't shut, on account of the body laying across the slick ground.

Her gaze flickered over the faded posters on the walls, the scattered papers that littered the desks – remnants of the police station's once orderly routine.

Abruptly, the hushed tension shattered. From the enveloping shadows, figures emerged, materializing like specters from the bowels of the precinct.

Doors slammed open in the back, near an office space. Figures responding to the gunshots from outside.

Momentarily, the incoming aggressors looked taken aback, as if they hadn't expected the threat to have reached the inside of the building. Dark suits clung to their broad frames, as if they were businessmen, but the gleam of cold metal in their hands betrayed their lethal intentions.

One shouted in Arabic, his voice echoing through the empty halls, transforming the silence.

Fifteen steps ahead, the first aggressor raised his gun. She was already closing the distance. She sidestepped swiftly as the first attacker fired. A loud *crack*. Something warm whizzed by her arm. Two more steps, and she was on him before he could fire again. Her arm shot out, hand slapping the gun aside while her other raised her Glock.

The report of her weapon was a harsh drumbeat in the confined space, a precise rhythm she dictated. One, two shots, each finding its mark, and the assailant crumpled to the ground in the doorway of the office space.

Two more figures emerged from the office to her left.

An aggressor swept in from her left, a knife glinting in the sterile light, Anna ducked, and the blade whistled over her head, a deadly arc missing its target. In one smooth motion, she pivoted on her heel, her own knife – a compact, serrated Karambit – appeared in her hand as if by magic.

Her assailant barely had time to register the shift in tactics before Anna's blade sliced through the fabric of his suit, cutting a shallow but decisive line across his thigh. His shout of pain was cut short as she used his momentary imbalance to thrust him against the wall with a calculated blow from her shoulder.

Pain flared in her arm from the impact, but she didn't register it. She couldn't afford to. Instead, Anna turned, sensing the second man she'd spotted moving behind her, his shadow telegraphing his approach. She ducked, feeling the rush of air as a fist sailed over where her head had been a split second earlier.

With a swift uppercut, she struck the underside of his arm, numbing it, disrupting his next strike. He faltered, stumbling into a wooden desk, and she capitalized on the opening, driving the palm of her hand upward into his nose with bone-crunching force, the sound lost amidst the chaos.

Breath for breath, heartbeat for heartbeat, she was not just defending herself; she was dismantling their resolve piece by piece.

Two bullets left.

Another man's head appeared from outside, this time. More gunmen rounding the side of the building. She fired twice.

He dropped.

She reached for a clip to reload.

But a final attacker emerged in the doorway, gaping at her, wide-eyed. A man with matted hair, and a golden tooth.

Anna's eyes, sharp as flint, darted the table at her side. A letter opener rested there. She didn't hesitate. The final attack shouted in Arabic, raised his gun. At the same time, her fingers wrapped around the cold metal of the opener.

She flung it, and he fired. His bullet went wide, as her profile was now turned towards him with the motion of the throw—the opener sliced through the air and found its mark in the hand of the nearest attacker. The weapon he held clattered to the floor, his cry of pain swallowed by the sudden silence.

All of this happened so quickly, she almost lost track of time, as if she'd been listening some lulling piece of music.

And then, she glanced back.

All the men dead or dying. Motionless.

All except one. The man who she'd slashed across the leg and shouldered into the wall. He was whimpering, stumbling away from her. He limped as he tried to escape.

She turned slowly.

Her footsteps like a judge's gavel. *Thump. Thump.*

He whimpered, panicked, trying to reach for a gun on the ground, but his fingers slick with his own blood. The gun fell.

This surviving man stared at her, panic in his eyes, horror forming his mouth into a small circle. He stammered a couple of times, glancing back, then at her again.

She didn't slow. Didn't speak.

He'd had his chance. Fatima never had a chance.

The world narrowed to the harsh echo of her own breaths and the closing footsteps of her final adversary. Anna's eyes, sharp as a hawk's despite the onslaught, caught the glint of aged plastic in the periphery—a relic from an era before pocket-sized technology dominated. The old hardwired phone sat squat on an adjacent desk, its coiled cord spiraling like a resting serpent.

He was trying to reach the phone.

She lunged, reaching it first.

Her fingers snaked around the receiver, the clammy press of the molded plastic grounding her fleeting senses. She whipped the cord around his neck.

He tried to slam into her, in a final, desperate bid.

But the assailant's momentum worked against him, the sharp jerk of the make-shift garrote cutting off his windpipe. His blood-slicked hand clawed at his throat, grappling for air that wouldn't come. Anna's grip remained merciless, unwavering until the twitching ceased and the body slumped, an inert mass.

Panting, every breath a blade in her side, Anna crumpled beside the fallen foe. Her limbs sprawled awkwardly on the cool linoleum, her back against the unforgiving edge of a desk. The chorus of battle faded from her ears, replaced now by the rush of her pulse, a frenetic beat.

And then...

The shrill ring of the phone cleaved through the stillness, an unexpected intruder.

She tensed.

The phone rang again.

She frowned at the landline, staring. Anna's hand, slick with exertion and speckled with the crimson of confrontation, twitched around the vintage plastic, its sudden animation a jarring dissonance against the heavy silence.

She swallowed once.

Riiing.

Riiing. Riiing.

The phone continued to pester her.

She frowned, glancing once more to the door of the police station. The men on the ground weren't cops. So why were they here?

Why had he sent them?

Sahid.

The name echoed along with the ringing phone.

She swallowed, wetted her lips, and then she reached out, snatching the phone off the wall and pressing it to her ear. "What?"

Chapter 18

The handset was slick with Anna's perspiration, pressed hard enough against her cheek that the plastic creaked. Her breath came in raw, ragged gasps, echoing slightly in the cramped space. Around her feet, the motionless bodies of Sahid's men lay scattered like discarded playthings. The acrid smell of gunpowder still hung in the air, mingling with the coppery scent of blood that splattered across the faded wallpaper.

"Hello, stranger," the voice crooned from the other end, "you're quite the artist, aren't you?"

She tensed at the sound, an almost feminine lilt that danced through the static of the line. It was a melody of menace, each note carefully played to unsettle and unnerve. The sing-song cadence hinted at a life cushioned by luxury, the kind that never knew the sting of hardship or the taste of fear—unless it was inflicted upon others.

Anna remained quiet, her grip on the phone tighter, the heavy breathing the only evidence of the storm raging within her. The man on the other end paused, likely picturing her amidst his fallen henchmen, awaiting her response with a perverse anticipation. But Anna knew better than to give him the satisfaction. She steadied her breathing, focusing past the lilting voice to the silence that might yield a clue, any clue.

"Who might you be, my dear?" The voice pirouetted out of the receiver, each word a calculated step in his verbal waltz. An accent. Not heavy, but obvious. She knew the voice. She'd heard it before in a briefing room once upon a time.

Anna's jaw clenched, her silence a fortress against his probing. She could almost hear the smirk that must have been spreading across his face, a predator amused by the prey caught in its snare.

"Ah, but why so quiet? Is it regret, perhaps?" he teased, his tone dripping with mock sympathy. "Or is it fear? You know, I have something very precious to you."

The room seemed to close in on Anna, every word from the man like a tightening vice. Her mind raced, but her features remained an impassive mask. There was little doubt that he would use whatever leverage he sought to twist the knife further.

He was fishing. He didn't know her. Didn't know who she was, but he was trying to find out. In the way she listened, trying to pick up on background noise—some clue—he also listened.

"Your silence won't protect them," he continued, his voice now a velvet threat. "I can assure you, my dear, pain has been... a guest in their company."

"Where are you?" she asked, the question not so much spoken as it was carved from ice.

"Such directness," the sing-song voice on the other end tittered. "But I'm curious about you. Tell me, why are you interested in my whereabouts?"

"Curiosity is a human trait," Anna replied, her voice low and even as if discussing the weather rather than negotiating with a serpent. "Why visit the US?"

She already knew the answer. The casino. Billions of dollars funneled through, funding who knew what hellish enterprises.

Her mind worked furiously behind the facade, each word measured, each pause calculated. She needed him talking, needed him unwittingly painting the picture of his hideout with every syllable he uttered.

"Ah, the land of opportunity," he crooned, almost as if savoring a fine wine. "One should always explore new ventures, don't you think?"

"Depends on the venture. Business or pleasure?"

"Perhaps a bit of both," came the coy response. He was enjoying this, the cat to her mouse, unaware that this mouse had claws sharp enough to tear through the veil he hid behind.

"Must be quite the change from back home," she pressed on, her tone casual but insistent.

Anna's grip on the phone tightened, the plastic creaking under the strain. She could hear the amusement woven through his words like poison in honey.

"Such a curious cat could end up in trouble, you know? Maybe even lose one of its nine lives."

Her jaw clenched, but she remained silent, her breath steady despite the pounding of her heart. Anna knew the game; she'd played it before and won.

"Or perhaps," he continued, stretching out his vowels, "it's not curiosity that drives you? What are you willing to do, to save someone you love? Is that what this is about? Have I hurt someone you love? A sister? A daughter? Hmm? Not a brother, surely."

Her fingers curled into a fist, the only sign of the frustration boiling within her as his voice filled the room, smooth and unyielding. Yet, all she heard beyond his words was the sterile silence of a dead line—no shuffling of henchmen, no distant street noise, nothing.

"Actions speak louder than words," she replied calmly, her own voice betraying none of the tension that knotted her muscles.

"Indeed," he purred, "and your actions have been... quite disruptive. But we know how to break unruly mares, don't we?"

She ignored the bait, her senses straining against the void of sound, searching for something—anything.

Her breaths came in measured puffs as she leaned closer to the mouthpiece. "I know who you are, Abdo Sahid," she breathed out, the syllables of the name hanging heavy in the air.

There was a palpable shift on the line—a sudden quiet that stretched into a chasm of silence. The humming of the connection became a tinnitus in Anna's ear.

Anna waited, patient as a spider in the center of its web, feeling the vibrations of the thread she'd plucked.

Then, softly at first, like a secret being whispered through the ages, the sound came. A distant whinny sliced through the stillness, a sharp contrast to the man's earlier silky tones. It was brief, almost lost beneath the layers of hissing static, but it was there, unmistakable.

Her eyes narrowed, a hunter catching the scent of its quarry. She recalled with vivid clarity the metaphor he had used before, about breaking women—as if they were wild mares to be tamed. It couldn't be a coincidence, not with Sahid. He was deliberate.

The realization struck a chord in her, resonating with the adrenaline that began to surge through her veins. Horses. She was sure of it now; he was near them. Her mind worked furiously, mapping out places, stables, farms—anywhere that could house such animals within his sphere of influence.

Anna's pulse quickened, her grip on the receiver tightening as if it were a lifeline. She could almost smell the fresh hay and leather through the phone, the images conjured by that single equine cry swirling into focus.

Sahid's voice finally slithered through, each syllable measured, insinuating. "Either way, you've signed their death warrant."

"You don't have anyone I love."

"And yet even now you want to save them. Who are you? Who is it? A sister? Must be. You sound young."

"No one. But threats are the resort of a desperate man."

There was a beat, a hitch in his breath that she caught as clearly as the scent of blood in water.

"Desperation?" Sahid chuckled, though the sound held no mirth, only a chilling promise. "No, my dear. This is simply amusement. But continue to entertain me, and I might consider a reprieve for your beloved."

"Consider all you like," Anna countered, her words sharp as daggers. "But remember, for every moment you waste, I am closing in. And when I find you—"

"Ah, but you won't." His interruption was swift, a razor slicing through her threat. "And just to ensure your cooperation, know this: your friend, your family—they will expire long before you even catch a glimpse of my shadow." A pause. "I don't know which of my new merchandise has caused this disruption. I suppose I'll just have to terminate all of them!" his voice cracked like a jockey's whip.

The line went dead, the hum of the dial tone mocking her in its monotony. Silence enveloped her once more, but now it was a different kind—a silence filled with the echo of his words and the unyielding tick of the clock.

He thought she was the family member of one of his victims. Likely, he'd faced crusaders before.

But he was wrong... And they were going to suffer for it.

Whoever he had recently brought in. She shivered, wondering how many women she'd just endangered.

Anna's hand clenched around the receiver, her knuckles blanching. The dial tone droned on, an endless loop. She stood motionless amidst the carnage she had wrought, the pale light from the moon casting long shadows across the room. The silence was a vacuum, and in it, Sahid's final words reverberated.

She slowly placed the phone back onto its cradle, the click sounding unnaturally loud in the tomb-like quiet.

She paused, thinking.

But no time.

She broke into a dead sprint.

Chapter 19

Anna's fingers danced over the screen, the soft glow of her phone the only light in the murky shadows of the alleyway. The digital map blinked into existence, pinpointing a pulsing red dot amidst a labyrinth of roads. Sahid's location locked in. The race track.

She hesitated, staring at the screen. A guess, but an educated one. Multiple news sources said overseas money had been invested here. Recently. Around the same time Sahid would've started showing interest in Vegas.

She didn't have time to follow the money. The women didn't have time.

She adjusted her body armor and shifted the shoulder strap for the rifle she'd borrowed from the police station's armory.

Grenades on her belt, and a machine gun in her hands. She wasn't here to play nice.

She checked her location once more, determining she'd arrived at the correct spot. She peered through the window, eyes narrowed.

She slipped the device into the pocket of her tactical vest, the action seamless, as if muscle memory alone guided her. Her breath was a steady rhythm in the chill night air.

The race track loomed ahead, a colossal giant slumbering under the moon's watchful eye, its sprawling expanse deserted at this late hour. But Anna knew better than to trust appearances; dangers often lurked in the quietest of places.

She surveyed the perimeter, every sense attuned to the task at hand as she moved away from the stolen cop car. Not a stray sound escaped her notice, not a single shift in the shadows went unseen.

Grenades nestled in pouches against her thigh, their weight a grim comfort, and strapped across her back, the sleek lines of a machine gun and a sniper rifle. The sniper an old, familiar friend. It eased her to feel its touch, like a security blanket rubbed against a child's face.

Anna moved with a ghost's whisper, her combat boots finding purchase on the gritty asphalt with nary a sound. She navigated through the gates, a shadow amongst shadows, her form blending seamlessly into the dark tapestry of the night. Each step was a calculated risk, each breath a countdown to confrontation.

The race track stretched before her now, an open expanse begging for the thunder of hooves and the roar of crowds. But tonight, it would bear witness to a different kind of contest.

Her finger caressed the cold metal of her sniper rifle as if it were an old lover.

The stillness of the race track was a deceit.

There, just beyond the reach of the ambient light that bled from the grandstand, the night was punctured by the muffled cries—distant yet piercing—a chorus of desperation that rose and fell with the wind.

She pressed forward, her body low and agile, ducking between the dilapidated betting booths and abandoned concession stands. The screams grew clearer, more distinct, each one a serrated edge scraping against her.

Then she saw them, silhouettes against the moonlit track—men armed to the teeth, their postures relaxed but vigilant. They were laughing, a guttural sound that twisted the night into something grotesque. As Anna crept closer, shards of Arabic sliced through the quiet.

"Yaktuluhum." Kill them.

The command was casual, as if they discussed the weather.

She lingered in the shadows, staring at the group of huddled men. Ten... fifteen she counted.

A fat man was shaking his head, holding a walkie-talkie to his sweaty check. In Arabic, he said, "We'll kill them. Just give us a second." He lowered the radio. A couple of thick-skulled men at his side watched the fat man, waiting for orders.

"Boss wants the merchandise extinguished."

The guards frowned. "After the race?"

The fat man waved a hand. "Why not? I've got money on this."

Anna peered over the railing, still sticking to the shadows. And there, far below, she spotted the race track. Her blood went cold. Young women were being pushed and whipped by men who laughed. The women were in tattered clothing, many of them looking as if they hadn't eaten for days. They left bloody footprints as they stumbled around the track. The men in the stands cheered. The men with the whips taunted.

Anna felt sick.

And now, it sounded like once the race was over, the lives of the women would also be forfeit.

She counted twenty men in total on the track and in the stands. All of them armed. No sign of Sahid. Normally, she'd gather intel. She'd find the location of a primary target. But now...

Things were different. Washington was no longer calling the shots.

She watched as one of the women stumbled, screaming. She was half-dressed, tears in her eyes, a hand upraised, but the captors laughed. A man whipped her. Again. Again.

He screamed at her to rise.

She pleaded.

He whipped her again. Another woman tried to interfere, to help.

But she received a beating for her efforts.

Anna watched with a cold, deadly detachment.

And so she made her own choice, emerging from the dark, her eyes fixated on the gathered men.

The muzzle of Anna's machine gun whispered death as she squeezed the trigger, a silent promise to those whose voices had been stolen. Bullets threaded through the air, stitching a path of finality across the chests of the men.

Voices shouted. Men turned to face her, their own weapons rising. But she was moving, fast. The gun she'd chosen was a machine gun. Specifically, an Austrian-designed 7.62mm machine gun. It fired rounds at a rate of 750 per minute. That was more than ten rounds a second. One moment, souls standing, taunting. The next... down like bowling pins.

The men didn't stand a chance. In the blink of an eye, Anna had moved from one end of the race track to the other, her gun chattering as she went. The echoes of the gunfire bounced off the grandstand and the distant buildings, enhancing the scene's chaos.

As the bullets tore into their bodies, the men tried to retreat, but Anna was too swift. One by one, they fell, their bodies twitching and then still.

Screams became background noise to the percussion of gunfire.

And then...

Silence.

Fifteen men lay scattered across the stands like morbid milestones; their intentions extinguished by her unwavering purpose.

With the immediate threat neutralized, Anna shifted positions. She found a vantage point where the moonlight painted a clearer picture of the remaining threats from the race track below, near the women. Her fingers worked deftly, assembling the sniper with practiced ease, the action as familiar as breathing.

Through the scope, the world reduced itself to simple decisions: breathe, aim, shoot. The cold eye of the lens focused on the men who still lurked at the periphery, the delay in their movements reflecting their confusion from the sudden onslaught.

Anna exhaled, the breath leaving her body in a controlled release as she squeezed the trigger once more. The sound of the sniper rifle's report was a solitary thunderclap, echoing off the grandstands, heralding an end to another life.

One by one, they fell—the guardians of terror now the victims of their own malice. Each pull of the trigger was a silent vow fulfilled, each bullet a whisper of justice for those who had suffered.

The final man on the track fell. The women were on the ground, cowering, terrified.

Anna wanted to console them, but she was moving again. Swift, like a specter.

The echo of gunfire receded, surrendering to a haunting silence that blanketed the racetrack. Anna's eyes, steely and sharp behind the scope, scanned for movement with predatory precision. The night air carried the soft whimpers of hidden souls to her ears—women, their spirits fractured by terror, sobbed in the shadowy crevices of the grandstand.

Amidst the fading cries, a singular figure emerged from the dimly lit underbelly. The man who'd been on the radio—a man of considerable girth, his chest heaving as he surveyed the carnage. His hands were empty, and his chest was covered in blood. He blinked, stumbled, and gasped as he hit the ground.

She turned, frowning at him.

Anna's finger rested lightly against the trigger, the sniper's muzzle tracking the fat man's path. He paused, wiping sweat from his brow with the back of his hand, oblivious to the crosshairs that held him in an invisible grip. She could sense his desperation, see it in the way his eyes darted about, searching for the angel of death who had decimated his ranks.

Anna strode across the pockmarked concrete, her boots pressing into the grit that had once seen the thunderous patter of hooves and cheers of onlookers. Now, it was a graveyard of spent cartridges and the echoes of recent violence. The fat man's sweat-slicked skin glistened in the weak light as she moved towards him.

Her feet tapped quietly against the dusty ground.

"Where is Sahid?" Her voice, a blade itself, cut through the lingering gun smoke.

He swallowed hard, his jowls quivering, and shook his head vehemently, too gripped by dread to muster words. His eyes were wide, the whites stark against the dirt smeared across his face.

"Speak," she commanded, stepping closer, her shadow enveloping him like an ominous shroud.

The fat man mumbled something unintelligible, his gaze skittering away from hers, fixated on the lethal calm in her poise.

"Your men are gone," Anna said, stating the evident truth as her hand slid to her belt, withdrawing a knife with a deliberate slowness designed to terrify. "You can join them, or you can talk."

She crouched beside him, the knife's blade catching a glint of light as she brought it near his throat. The fat man's breathing hitched, a bead of perspiration trailing down his temple, soaking into the collar of his shirt.

"Announcer's box," he gasped suddenly, pointing with a trembling sausage-like finger towards the dilapidated structure looming over the racetrack. His eyes never left the gleaming steel at his neck, reflecting his own petrified image back at him.

"Good choice," Anna murmured, her tone devoid of warmth. She didn't lower the knife immediately, letting the threat hang between them for a heartbeat longer, etching the gravity of the situation into the fat man's consciousness. Only when his fear was palpable, a tangible taste in the air, did she retract the blade and slip it back into its sheath.

With a nod, Anna rose to her feet, leaving the fat man to ponder the thin slice of fate that had spared him—for the moment. Her focus shifted to the announcer's box; the next stage of her hunt just within sight.

The structure stood ominously against the twilight sky. She took one stealthy step forward, then another, her body tense.

Without warning, the air cracked with a gunshot, the sound ricocheting off the desolate grandstands. Pain seared through Anna's shoulder, and instinctively, she twisted away from the bullet's burning kiss, collapsing onto the cold, gritty asphalt. Her breath hitched in her chest, a sharp contrast to the silence that had abruptly reclaimed the racetrack.

Gritting her teeth against the throbbing wound, Anna rolled to cover, her fingers trembling as they pressed against the warmth soaking through her shirt. She cast a quick glance at the torn fabric, the raw flesh beneath it weeping crimson. Anger flared within her, not just at the injury but at the realization that Sahid was shooting at her.

With her free hand, she retrieved her sniper rifle. The announcer's box presented itself as a patchwork of shadows and faded paint, a hideout for cowards.

There, a subtle movement—a glint of metal where no light should be. Anna's finger caressed the trigger, her heartbeat slowing even as adrenaline surged through her veins. She exhaled slowly, the crosshairs dancing over the slim aperture in the box's facade where the shooter lay in wait.

She'd somehow found herself in a sniper's standoff.

Chapter 20

Sparks flew off the concrete barricade as bullets hammered into it, chipping away at Anna's scant cover. Her breaths came out in controlled bursts, each one syncing with the lull between gunfire.

With a predator's grace, she rolled to her left, the movement so fluid it seemed choreographed. A fraction of a second was all she needed to lock onto her first target. The rifle recoiled against her shoulder as she squeezed the trigger. A shadow in the window of the announcer's box spun. A chair. Not a body. Shit. With the glass shattered now, it was more evident.

She couldn't stay in one place.

Without hesitation, Anna slid across the floor to another piece of cover—an overturned table—her movements a blur. Muscle memory guided her actions; this dance with death was one she had performed countless times.

The acrid scent of gunpowder stung the air, mingling with her adrenaline. Her senses were heightened to a supernatural degree, every sound, every shift in the shadows registered and calculated with cold efficiency.

She advanced, her boots silent on the dirt-strewn ground, her every step measured and deliberate. She moved towards the announcer's box now. Down a set of stairs, along the path leading around the track, towards the elevated position. She ducked behind a stack of metal chairs just as lead peppered where she had stood moments before.

From this new angle, she could see two more of Sahid's men closing in, their rifles scanning for any sign of her. But Anna was a ghost, unseen until she wanted to be. In a swift motion, she popped up from her shelter, her finger applying just enough pressure to the trigger. Two shots rang out in quick succession, and two bodies thudded onto the dusty floor.

The crackle of the intercom shattered the rhythm of gunfire, Sahid's voice slithering through the chaos like a viper. "Hello, stranger," he cooed mockingly, each syllable dripping with malice. "Playing the hero once again? But how heroic will you feel when innocent blood stains your hands?"

His threat hung in the stale air, as palpable as the smoke that curled from the barrel of her rifle. Below her, the women, hostages of this mad game, crouched and trembled. Anna's heart pounded against her ribcage, not solely from the exertion but from the weight of the decision that now clawed at her conscience.

She pressed her back against the cold concrete, the rough texture a stark contrast to the slick fear that coated her skin. To remain hidden could spell a massacre for those she had sworn to protect.

"Tick-tock," Sahid taunted, his voice echoing off the walls, a predator toying with its prey. "How long will you cower? Your silence is their demise."

Anna's jaw clenched, the taste of iron and resolve mixing on her tongue. She eyed the expanse of open ground between her and the next cover—a graveyard sprint if she mistimed it. Her fingers tightened around her rifle.

In the shuddering breaths between shots, she weighed her life against the lives of many. The scales tipped, her duty clear, yet every instinct screamed to stay concealed, to survive, to fight another day. But the piercing cries of fear below snuffed out the siren call of self-preservation. Sahid's game was one of terror, and Anna knew the cost of playing it safe. Too damn high.

"Come out, come out, wherever you are," Sahid sang, his voice a poisoned lullaby. "Or I start mowing them down. Isn't that the expression?"

With a silent prayer, she readied herself.

A sharp crack shattered the ominous silence, followed by a harrowing scream that sliced through Anna's composure. Below on the track, a woman clutched her leg, crimson blooming across her white shorts as she collapsed. The others scattered like leaves in a gust of wind, their footsteps erratic drumbeats against the dirt.

"Tick-tock," Sahid's voice slithered through the intercom. "Every moment you hide, another one pays the price."

Anna's breath hitched, her heart thundering against her ribcage. She couldn't see him, but she felt his eyes, imagined the cold glint behind his scope. Her fingers danced along the rifle's barrel, each second feeling an eternity, each heartbeat a gavel judging her indecision.

"Isn't this thrilling?" His tone was light, mocking, yet laden with an undercurrent of malice. "The protector, frozen while the innocent suffer. How does it feel? Knowing their pain is on your hands?"

His words were a vice around her mind, tightening with every inflection, every syllable designed to unnerve. He wanted her frazzled, reactionary.

"Heroes are so predictable," he continued, the smirk in his voice unmistakable. "Always willing to sacrifice themselves for the greater good. But I wonder, dear, where is your limit? Make your move, or I make mine," Sahid prodded, his patience thinning.

"Enough!" Anna hissed under her breath, fury lacing the word.

She pulled back from her scope, taking a moment to survey the broader scene, allowing her tactical mind to override the visceral images that threatened to cloud her judgment. Options flickered through her thoughts, each discarded as quickly as it arose—too risky, too slow, too uncertain.

Then, amidst the turmoil, an idea sparked. It was audacious, bordering on reckless, but it carried the faintest glimmer of possibility.

Ignoring the bile rising in her throat, Anna seized the fleeting strategy, her mind racing to assemble the pieces. She would need to be swift, precise. There was no room for error—not with Sahid's expertise.

Her breaths came out in measured beats as she leaned away from the barricade, hands inching toward the sky—a universal gesture that spoke louder than any plea for parley. She stepped into the open, the moon harsh against her skin, the grit beneath her boots grounding her to the moment.

Each step was a calculated risk, a deliberate stride into the lion's den, but Anna's gaze remained unflinching. She could feel Sahid's sniper scope trained on her, the crosshairs dancing over her heart, yet it was the thought of those innocent lives that kept her legs moving, her resolve unwavering. She reached down, and pulled her shirt up and off.

She dropped it.

She wore a sports bra, and her lithe form was scarred and muscled.

But she knew men like Sahid. She just needed to get close enough. He was a man of indulgence—a man of depravity. The sight alone would titillate him. She approached, moving slowly, shirtless now, hands raised, and aware that she was risking her life on a lecherous man's inability to control his lust.

"Bravo," Sahid's voice crackled from the intercom, laced with mock applause. "The martyr emerges."

She halted, arms still raised, exposed and vulnerable amidst the desolation of the track—her surrender a stark contrast to the chaos that had reigned moments before. Here she was, the last gambit laid bare, trading herself for time, for lives, for a chance.

Anna's jaw clenched, the muscles twitching with the strain of her silence. She could almost picture Sahid's smug grin, the self-assured tilt of his head as he peered down at her from his unseen perch.

"Let them go, Sahid," Anna called out, her voice a blend of command and concession, carrying across the expanse.

The intercom crackled again, and there was a hush—a void filled with nothing but the anticipation of Sahid's reply and the distant sobs of the frightened women.

She took a step forward, then another, her hands slowly lowering as she approached the entrance to the announcer's box.

And still, he didn't shoot.

She'd been right. At least for now. He was watching, ogling... and for the moment, he allowed her closer... closer... and closer still.

Chapter 21

Anna's silhouette merged with the darkness, her breath steady in the hush of twilight. As she stepped into the murky light cast by a flickering race-track lamp, she raised her hands, palms open and exposed to the starry sky. Her movements were deliberate, a silent offering of peace to the figure waiting across the desolate racetrack.

"See, Sahid? No tricks," she called out, her voice laced with a feigned vulnerability that belied the steel in her spine. "Like what you see?" she taunted, using his momentary lapse to solidify her advantage.

Sahid's voice sliced through the tension-charged silence, a sharpness edged with derision. "Come on then. Do you honestly expect me to fall for this little show?"

Anna's fingers, cool and steady, slipped into the deep pockets of her cargo pants. Beneath the fabric, her touch grazed the cold metal of the grenades, their weight reassuring against her palms. With the finesse of a magician concealing a trick, she palmed them, her skin brushing against the grooved surface, the pins snug under her grip.

"Wouldn't dream of it," she murmured, more to herself than to Sahid. Her heart thrummed a rhythm, but her hands betrayed no tremor.

And then, she spotted the figure. He couldn't resist. He wanted to see her. To toy with her.

The man was as ugly as she remembered: pockmarked, greasy hair, beady eyes darting between her and his scope. Sahid.

The corners of Sahid's mouth twitched upwards in anticipation, expecting her compliance. He stood in a shattered window, peering down at her.

Her boots left shallow impressions in the dirt, marking her path towards destiny's fulcrum. The air around her seemed to hold its breath, charged with the static of impending reckoning. In the vast expanse of the field, Anna found her stage, the center where every echo would find its way back to its source.

She halted, her position calculated, equidistant from the track's abandoned bleachers and the skeletal remains of the announcer's booth.

Sahid's voice slithered through the darkness, its venomous tone meant to unnerve. "You're out of your depth, little girl." His rifle pointed at her chest.

The mocking words hovered in the air, but Anna remained still. The disdain in Sahid's voice was designed to rattle her. It didn't.

"A pretty thing like you shouldn't play with the big boys," he continued, his laughter a discordant note. His accent grew thicker the more he taunted.

She didn't flinch, not even at the baiting. Instead, she raised her head, her gaze piercing through the shadows toward the booth where Sahid perched like a vulture awaiting carrion. The floodlights cast sharp angles across his face, illuminating the smug assurance that had become his trademark.

Sahid's features, so familiar to Anna, contorted with the ugly twist of his ego. She knew that look, had seen it before on faces of those who thought they held all the cards.

In that prolonged gaze, Anna read his arrogance like an open book, each taunt fueling her. Her chest tightened, not with fear, but with the pump of adrenaline that came before the strike.

There was no doubt left in her mind; there was only the mission and the man who needed to be stopped.

His underestimation was his folly, and her weapon. She let the corners of her lips twitch, almost imperceptibly.

"Too late," she called. In one fluid motion, Anna drew her arms back and then forward, releasing the grenades into a graceful arc.

They spun through the air, twin harbingers, catching the light as they sailed toward the unsuspecting Sahid. His momentary distraction, that split-second glance away from his prey to indulge in his own hubris, left him vulnerable. It was all the opening Anna needed.

In the silence between breaths, the women on the track held their collective breath, their eyes tracing the path of the flying grenades as if tethered to them by invisible strings.

Sahid's laughter, a melody of scorn and malice, curdled in his throat as the pinprick glints of metal caught the moon's light. His features, once twisted into a sneer, stretched wide with the dawning horror of realization. The world around him, the field, the onlookers, the very air he breathed, all congealed into a viscous sludge, time oozing to a crawl.

His pupils dilated, eclipsing the arrogant gleam that had resided there seconds before. Chest heaving, muscles tensed like a cornered animal, Sahid could only watch as the inevitable approached.

With the reflexes of one who'd danced with death more times than he cared to count, Sahid threw himself backward. It was an instinct, primal and terrified. But it didn't matter. She'd cooked the frags before launching them.

A bloom of orange and red unfurled, a furious flower of flames erupting where Sahid had been moments ago. The shockwave that followed punched the air, sending out a blast. She glimpsed his form ripped to shreds, his body bursting into grisly debris. The announcer's booth became a pyre—its timber and steel contorting in the impromptu inferno.

Anna stood her ground, her silhouette etched against the bursting glow of fire. She watched as Sahid's sanctuary disintegrated.

The heat of the blast licked at her skin, yet she did not flinch.

Chapter 22

Anna sat in her RV, wincing as she wrapped the bandage around her shoulder once more, and then reaching out to take the binoculars from Waldo.

Reluctantly, he handed them over. She watched as the women were led, one at a time, into the waiting ambulances. One woman paused, looking around. She swallowed, glancing towards the RV. Her eyes met Anna's, even at this great distance.

"Jacinth Meek?" asked a paramedic, her voice faint in the distance as she read off a clipboard. The young woman named Jacinth stammered, nodded, and looked away again.

Anna stared at this young woman, watchful. "That one's a fighter," she said simply.

Waldo just grunted.

Anna waited until the last of the women had been placed in an ambulance, and only then did she lower her binoculars, hand them to Waldo and gun the engine.

"So..." he said carefully. "That briefcase full of money..."

"Gone," she said simply.

"Shit. Wanna stop at a casino on the way back?"

"No."

She turned onto the main road. Ahead, she spotted a row of black vehicles coming towards her. She winced as they flew past. Through the open window of the leading SUV, she thought she spotted the familiar faces of Greeves and Jefferson. Anna ducked her head as she sped past them. As she checked her mirror, she let out a slow breath of relief.

The feds weren't turning around.

At least for now, they were too busy—too distracted—just like Sahid had been. They wanted to collect the pieces of the human trafficker, and she couldn't blame them. Waldo was prattling again, so Anna reached out and turned on the radio.

A classic rock song came on, the guitar riff familiar and comforting in the wake of the destruction they'd just witnessed. Anna absentmindedly tapped her fingers along to the beat, the rhythm a soothing counterpoint to the adrenaline still coursing through her veins. She glanced at Waldo, who was staring out the window, a furrowed brow betraying his own thoughts.

"You thinking about Sahid?" Anna asked quietly.

Waldo turned to look at her, his eyes narrowing. "I'm thinking about how we're going to get out of this mess. I'm on the federal radar now. Those feds are going to be after us, and they're not going to stop until they've got us in cuffs."

Anna's lips twitched into a grim smile. "Maybe." She gestured to the radio, the music still playing in the background.

Waldo hesitated, swallowed. "You enjoyed that."

"Hmm?"

"All that, back there. You enjoyed it."

She glanced at him, then back at the road.

"And they call me the criminal..."

She frowned but didn't reply. She didn't see the point.

As they drove deeper into the heartland, the radio station they had been listening to faded into a static hum, the classic rock song replaced by an eerie silence.

Anna was lost in her thoughts, her gaze fixed on the horizon. She about to reach out and turn the radio back on, but decided against it. There was something comforting about the silence, a rare moment of tranquility.

"You know… I think I know someone who might help."

Anna glanced at him. "How's that?"

"To find out…" he swallowed. "About Beth's family. I know someone who might help."

She stared at him, and he shouted suddenly, reaching out and yanking the steering wheel to veer them back into their lane.

A moment later, their tires screeched against the asphalt.

"What are you talking about?"

"Holy shit, you trying to get us killed?"

"I had it handled. What are you talking about."

"Give me a sec. Holy…" he exhaled slowly.

"Waldo. Talk."

Waldo waved a hand. "I know a guy. He's expensive. Really expensive… but… Casper mentioned you had access to those funds. The ones I helped get."

Anna glared. "Is this a play?"

"What? No! No... just trying to help."

"Because, I swear, if you're trying to play us, I'll bury you. Alive."

He wagged a finger over his heart. "Cross my heart. No play. Just, you know, tryna be helpful." He flashed an unnerving smile.

"So how come you didn't mention this guy before?"

"Didn't know you had that type of cash. I sure as hell don't."

Anna frowned. She wasn't sure she trusted Waldo. No... in fact, she was sure. She didn't.

But... if he was telling the truth. If they could find out, for sure, about Beth's family... Wasn't it worth the risk? But he was wrong... They didn't have those funds. They'd lost the briefcase to the albino.

But Waldo didn't need to know that.

They were now on the FBI's radar. But Anna's mind kept moving back to the albino. That psychopath who'd kidnapped Beth's family. There were more threats out there than just the feds.

She nodded once, flooring the gas as she tore through the night. "Tell me who this guy is. Can we trust him?"

"Nope. Not at all. She's extremely dangerous."

"She?"

"Yeah. Like I said... she's a killer. But, if you have enough money... she'll have answers. I think. Er, hope. As long as she doesn't shoot me on sight."

"That's a theme with people who know you, isn't it?"

"I have my charms."

Anna shook her head. "Tell me a name."

"O... okay. But, I'm warning you. You're not gonna like it."

The End.

Book 3 is waiting for you. Scan the QR code with your phone to find your copy of Guardian's Nemesis.

GUARDIAN'S WRATH

What's Next for Anna Gabriel?

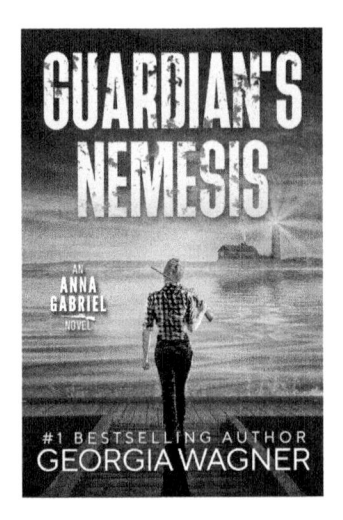

In the quiet, seemingly idyllic town of Clearwater, Maine, ex-Navy SEAL sniper Anna Gabriel seeks solace from her tumultuous past. Having operated in the shadows of black ops, she yearns for nothing but a peaceful life away from the chaos and violence that once defined her. However, Clearwater harbors secrets darker than anything she has faced on foreign soil.

When the town's beloved mayor is found dead under mysterious circumstances, Anna's attempt at a quiet life is shattered. Rumors of foul play swirl, pointing toward the town's wealthiest and most influential family, the Harringtons, whose patriarch has long sought to control every aspect of Clearwater's day-to-day life. As Anna reluctantly uses her unique skills to investigate, she uncovers a web of corruption, greed, and betrayal that threatens to consume the town.

But the Harringtons are not her only concern. A figure from Anna's black ops past, known only as "The Phantom," has tracked her to Clearwater. This ghost from her past is both a formidable ally and a dangerous nemesis, whose motives are as mysterious as his identity.

Also by Georgia Wagner

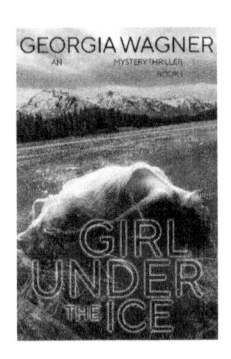

Once a rising star in the FBI, with the best case closure rate of any investigator, Ella Porter is now exiled to a small gold mining town bordering the wilderness of Alaska. The reason for her new assignment? She allowed a prolific serial killer to escape custody.

But what no one knows is that she did it on purpose.

The day she shows up in Nome, bags still unpacked, the wife of the richest gold miner in town goes missing. This is the second woman to vanish in as many days. And it's up to Ella to find out what happened.

Assigning Ella to Nome is no accident, either. Though she swore she'd never return, Ella grew up in the small, gold mining town, treated like royalty as a child due to her own family's wealth. But like all gold tycoons, the Porter family secrets are as dark as Ella's own.

Also by Georgia Wagner

The skeletons in her closet are twitching...

Genius chess master and FBI consultant Artemis Blythe swore she'd never return to the misty Cascade Mountains.

Her father—a notorious serial killer, responsible for the deaths of seven women—is now imprisoned, in no small part due to a clue she provided nearly fifteen years ago.

And now her father wants his vengeance. A new serial killer is hunting the wealthy and the elite in the town of Pinelake. Artemis' father claims he knows the identity of the killer, but he'll only tell daughter dearest. Against her will, she finds herself forced back to her old stomping grounds.

Once known as a child chess prodigy, now the locals only think of her as 'The Ghostkiller's' daughter. In the face of a shamed family name and a brother involved with the Seattle mob, Artemis endeavours to use her tactical genius to solve the baffling case.

Hunting a murderer who strikes without a trace, if she fails, the next skeleton in her closet will be her own.

Also by Georgia Wagner

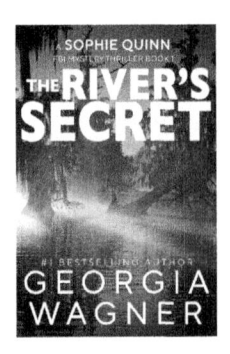

A cold knife, a brutal laugh.

Then the odds-defying escape.

Once a hypnotist with her own TV show, now, Sophie Quinn works as a full-time consultant for the FBI. Everything changed six years ago. She can still remember that horrible night. Slated to be the River Killer's tenth victim, she managed to slip her bindings and barely escape where so many others failed. Her sister wasn't so lucky.

And now the killer is back.

Two PHDs later, she's now a rising star at the FBI. Her photographic memory helps solve crimes, but also helps her to never forget. She saw the River Killer's tattoo. She knows what he sounds like. And now, ten years later, he's active again.

Sophie Quinn heads back home to the swamps of Louisiana, along the Mississippi River, intent on evening the score and finding the man who killed her sister. It's been six years since she's been home, though. Broken relationships and shattered dreams exist among the bayous, the rivers, the waterways and swamps of Louisiana; can Sophie find her way home again? Or will she be the River Killer's next victim to float downstream?

Want to know more?

Want to see what else the Greenfield authors have written? Go to the website.

https://greenfieldpress.co.uk/

Or sign up to our newsletter where you will get sneak peeks, exclusive giveaways, behind the scenes content, and more. Plus, you'll be notified of Fan Pricing events when they occur and get exclusive offers from other authors.

Copy the link into your web browser.

https://greenfieldpress.co.uk/newsletter/

Prefer social media? Join our thriving Facebook community.

Want to join the inner circle where you can keep up to date with everything? This is a free page on Facebook where you can hang out with likeminded individuals and enjoy discussing my books. There is cake too (but only if you bring it).

https://www.facebook.com/GreenfieldPress

About the Author

Georgia Wagner worked as a ghost writer for many, many years before finally taking the plunge into self-publishing. Location and character are two big factors for Georgia, and getting those right allows the story to flow seamlessly onto the page. And flow it does, because Georgia is so prolific a new term is required to describe the rate at which nerve-tingling stories find their way into print.

When not found attached to a laptop, Georgia likes spending time in local arboretums, among the trees and ponds. An avid cultivator of orchids, begonias, and all things floral, Georgia also has a strong penchant for art, paintings, and sculptures.

Printed in Dunstable, United Kingdom